HORSES

Keith Ridgway is from Dublin. This novella *Horses* first appeared in 1997 and was followed in 1998 by his critically acclaimed first novel *The Long Falling*, which has since been awarded both the prestigious Prix Femina Etranger and Premier Roman Etranger in France. His stories have appeared in various anthologies in Ireland, Britain and the United States. His most recent collection, *Standard Time*, won the Rooney Prize 2001, and his new novel, *The Parts*, is also published by Faber.

KEITH RIDGWAY

Horses

faber and faber

First published in 1997
as part of *First Fictions: Introduction 13*
by Faber and Faber Limited
3 Queen Square London WC1N 3AU
This paperback edition first published in 2003

Phototypeset by Intype London Ltd
Printed in England by Mackays of Chatham plc, Chatham, Kent

A CIP record for this book
is available from the British Library

ISBN 0–571–21645–5

2 4 6 8 10 9 7 5 3 1

For my sister Barbara

HORSES

In the broad spaces of the streets near the square, Mathew stood and watched for the secrets which the rain reveals. In the air around the mountains he could see the clouds begin to form, to gather themselves like skirts held in, to muster and breathe deep and peer down the slopes to the place where people live, and plot a route. He saw them set off then with a tiny roll, and saw them pick up speed and press a silence out in front of them, and pick up speed again and canter quietly, billowing, and roll on into a gallop like a charge of black and ghostly horses, their hooves turning in the air, churning up a grey dust against the sun.

Mathew scratched his head. The light dimmed slowly as he stood and waited, knowing that he was being watched lazily by the priest on the steps of the courthouse and the woman who sold fish from a cart by the graveyard.

'Christ,' hissed Mathew, as the first drops of rain hit the dust up by the burnt-out cinema where children chased a dog. Miss Helen was walking towards him, her forehead creased across the centre like a chop in a log.

'You Doyle, you,' she shouted, and Mathew could hear the priest giggle. 'You come here, you bucking flanker.'

He turned and broke into a trot, thinking that perhaps it was not bucking flanker that she had said exactly. The rain reached him now, and ran faster than he did, darkening his path in front of him.

'Stop, you flanker. You plastered and you boiled ham.'

Boiled ham? He twisted his little finger on his ear as he

ran and he increased his speed and glanced over his shoulder and saw her getting smaller at the corner where the butcher's had been before the fire. She had given up.

'I'll get you, you hunt arranger. Flanker!' she screamed after him. He stopped and put his hands on his knees and bent to catch his breath and felt the rain get powerful on the skin of his back.

'Christ,' he hissed again.

The sky was a fine black when he looked up, and the rain a gorgeous thing that turned the dust at his feet to mud that seeped over the skin of his toes like chocolate. He wiped his chest and watched as the rain ran over it again, taking strange routes down his stomach and disappearing into the gap of his big jeans, tickling him. He giggled and shuddered like a wet dog.

'What is it, Mathew? Never felt the rain before?'

He spun around and found the priest there, his bald head seeming to explode with little spurts of water, like the sprinkler in the garden of the big house by the lake.

'Father. Oh dear.'

'Don't worry, Mathew,' he said, taking Mathew by the arm and hurrying him along towards the church. 'We'll get you inside and find you some clothes.'

'Father. Oh dear.'

They jogged to the sacristy door through the noise of the rain, and the priest fumbled for a while with a key. They walked then into the silence and through the musty cold room where they kept the silver that held God's body, and the priest's robes that he wore at Mass, and the little white things that became God's body when the boy rang the bell and everyone bowed their heads. One time, though, Mathew had looked up and he had seen the Holy Spirit fly down through the roof and past the priest's head and into the big

4

white thing that the priest held up so that it glowed and shone out a light into all the other white things and into Mathew's heart and made him feel thirsty.

'Come on. Don't linger,' said the priest.

'Oh dear,' said Mathew.

They walked on into the church, dripping rain on the floor, coming out onto the side of the altar where Mathew had never been before. It made the church look different, seeing it from up here. It looked bigger, and he gasped a little.

'It's all right. Come on.'

The priest walked to the front of the altar and then across it, stopping and genuflecting in the middle. Mathew did the same, but he farted as his knee touched the ground, just a little one, but he clutched his mouth and felt himself turn red, and froze. He saw Jesus look down at him from the cross and he was struck by his eyes and he knew that he would never be able to move again, he would be paralysed and left there as a warning so that no one else would do that horrible thing in a church ever again.

'Come on, Mathew. Please.'

The priest took his arm and lifted him up and led him on, across the altar and out the side door and into the corridor that led to the priest's house.

'Oh dear, Father. Oh dear.'

'It's all right, Mathew.'

Inside, the priest sat him down in the kitchen and gave him a towel, and then thought better of it and led him to the bathroom and showed him where everything was and told him to have a shower in the bath and smiled and patted his back and left him then and Mathew could hear the radio come on back in the kitchen.

He took off his jeans and stepped into the bath and ran

the water and held the nozzle like the priest had shown him. It was cold at first and Mathew hooted, but then it warmed up and it was nice, the way it soothed his skin. He used the soap and got all soapy and laughed. Then he tried the shampoo that the priest had shown him, rubbing it into his hair. It ran down his face in bubbles and he laughed even more, but then he got some in his eyes and cried out and rubbed them with his fingers but that just made it worse and he thought that his eyes were being burned out of his head and he screamed and the priest came running in and told him to calm down, that it wouldn't do any harm, and he washed his eyes out with cold water and rinsed him off and gave him a big towel and told him to dry himself.

'Don't put on those jeans, though. I'll get you some nice clean things.'

He went out and Mathew dried himself well, rubbing the soft towel over his body and liking the way it made him warm on the inside as well.

The priest knocked on the door and Mathew held the towel around himself and said 'Come in, Father' and the priest came in and smiled and handed him a bundle and told him that he hoped everything fitted and that when he was dressed he was to come into the kitchen.

There was a pair of white underpants that were a little big, but it was nice to have underpants again and Mathew smiled. There was a T-shirt that was the right size. It had something written on it that was like a row of curled-up worms like there sometimes are in the mud by the lake. There were black trousers and Mathew frowned when he felt them because they were thin and wouldn't last long. But they fitted well. There was a white shirt that was very big, but Mathew tucked it in well and rolled up the sleeves a little and looked in the mirror and liked himself. He was handsome.

There were socks. He hadn't worn socks since he was little. He tried them on but didn't like the way they felt and took them off again and put them into the pockets of the trousers and ran his hands through his hair and went to the kitchen.

'Well, well, aren't you the business, eh?' said the priest and smiled and Mathew laughed.

'The business, Father.'

'Did you not put on the socks?'

'I'm not used to them, Father.'

The priest looked at him and nodded and smiled again.

'Well, sit down. Will you have a cup of tea?'

'Yes please, Father.'

Mathew sat at the table and kept his hands on his knees which was good manners. The rain was rattling against the window and Mathew stared at it for a moment and felt all the warmer for seeing it. The priest poured out a mug of tea and put a fat sandwich in front of him and then poured a mug for himself, but he had no sandwich.

'Eat up then, Mathew. I'm sure you're hungry.'

'Thank you, Father.'

He picked up the sandwich and bit into it and tasted onion and ham and cheese and other things that he could not name. As he chewed he felt the tastes whirl and mingle and he did not like some of them, bitter and small like a finger caught in a gate, and he made a face.

'Is it all right?'

'Blumley,' said Mathew, spitting coleslaw onto the priest's black jacket and shrieking inside when he saw it, and then realizing that he had his mouth open and it was full of food and he snapped it shut and bit his tongue.

'Cryseest!' he said and stopped everything and looked down and felt the pain in his mouth and his face turn a deep red.

'Sorry, Mathew,' said the priest, and out of the corner of his eye Mathew could see him wiping the coleslaw from his lapel. 'I shouldn't talk to you while you're eating.'

Slowly, as the pain died away, Mathew took up his eating again, and sipped at the tea. He was glad though when eventually the sandwich was finished and the priest put a great big slab of chocolate cake in front of him.

'Now that'll keep you happy.'

'Thank you, Father.'

It was lovely and rich and the cream on it was fresh and cool and it all mixed together in Mathew's mouth so well that he could forget the onion and could almost forget his tongue.

'Why was Miss Brooks shouting at you, Mathew?'

'Miss Helen?'

'Yes. Miss Helen.'

'I don't know, Father.'

The priest sipped his tea and ran his finger around the table gently, as if he was writing in the wood, and Mathew remembered that it was like what Jesus did when the woman was brought before him, and he wondered if the priest was like Jesus all the time or just when he had to be.

'She called you an arsonist, Mathew.'

Mathew stared at the priest. It wasn't like Jesus to use words like that.

'Do you know what arsonist means, Mathew?'

Mathew shook his head and felt himself turn red and hoped it was not going to be one of those conversations.

'An arsonist is somebody who lights fires. On purpose. Not a fire in the grate to keep warm by. I mean a fire that

8

burns down a building. Like what happened with the cinema and the butcher's and . . .'

Mathew said something and then couldn't remember what it was he had said.

'That's right,' said the priest.

'That's a bad business,' said Mathew.

'It is indeed, very bad.'

'I wouldn't do that, Father, I don't like the heat of big fires. A fire in the grate like you said is only as big as your feet or your face or the cold bits of you, but those big fires are bigger than all of you and I've never been that cold, Father.'

The priest rested his chin on his hand and looked at Mathew with solid eyes that made Mathew blink and rummage about in his mind for something else to tell him.

'Like the cinema, Father. That was an awful heat so that was. It was like a big mouth coming towards you, opened up and going to swallow you and you could feel it close about you and it was awful, Father. I ran and ran from that.'

'You were there, then, Mathew?'

The priest had lifted his chin a little from where his hand was and Mathew could see through the gap the little square of white in his collar like the first bit of paint on a black wall.

'Oh no, Father, I wasn't, I mean I saw the . . . I was, Father, yes.'

'That's all right, I'm not going to give out to you. You just tell me what you saw, will you?'

'I will, Father, yes.'

The rain was stopping now. There was no noise from the window, and just the odd drop hit the glass. Mathew could see a blue sky in the distance. He ran his sore tongue around his mouth, finding bits of cake and swallowing them.

'It was night time, Father, no moon, cloudy, no stars, black as your jacket, Father. And quiet too, not a sound to be heard, Father, no dogs or cats or night birds or people. Not a thing at all.'

Mathew closed his eyes to better remember.

'I was lain in the long grass out behind Mr Grealy's shop, up against the fence, with my legs in a sack that I'd found, Father, just found, on the road, that must have fallen from the coal cart, and my coat around me, dozing.'

'You have a coat, Mathew?'

'Oh yes, Father. I have a number of things. I have a coat and a pair of shoes and I have a scarf and a jumper with no arms on it and a little book and a tin mug and a knife as sharp as a razor and a soldier with a red jacket on him and his arms shaped for holding a gun, but no gun there – it must have fallen out sometime. And the sack, Father, for keeping it all in.'

'And where is all this?'

Mathew dropped his head. 'It's hidden, Father.'

'All right, that's all right. But would you not wear more, Mathew? Would you not wear the shoes?'

'In winter, Father. I wear the shoes in winter. And the jumper too. And the coat. I'm all wrapped up in winter.'

The priest smiled kindly and Mathew wondered whether he would be allowed to keep the shirt and the T-shirt and the new trousers. They would be good to have for special days.

'Well, go on,' said the priest. 'What happened?'

'What, Father?'

'The night of the fire, Mathew. You were dozing behind Grealy's. What happened next?'

'Well, Father, in all that quiet, and with nothing really for the eyes to see, you can hear an awful long way away. And

10

I heard these voices you see, passing by in the street in front of the shop. Men's voices, talking very low and strange, as if they were up to something, Father.'

'Did you recognize them?'

'No, Father, they were too far away. But I didn't like the sound of them, Father. They were like the voices of the men that beat me, and I was afraid of them.'

'What men beat you?'

'Oh, it was a long time ago, Father, before you came here. Mr O'Malley and his son and another man who's dead now who was called Billy Joyce came to me one night and kicked me and punched me and the young O'Malley went to the toilet on me.'

'Good God.'

'Yes, Father, it was awful. I lay there and couldn't move and it was old Mrs Murtagh, God rest her, who found me in the morning and called the doctor, Dr Brooks, and I was taken to the hospital in Dublin and I had to stay there for three days and the nurses were lovely and Garda Cullen came to see me to wish me well and he promised me that if I told him who had done it he would make sure that they'd be punished and that no more harm would come to me for telling him, and he was a lovely man Garda Cullen, so I told him what had happened. I don't know what he did but Billy Joyce left the town after that and moved out to Enniskerry and he died there the next year, hit by a truck, and the O'Malleys kept out of my way after that and even now when either of them sees me coming they cross the road and look awful shamefaced and nobody really talks to them since that. And Garda Cullen always told me not to let anyone do that kind of thing. He told me that sometimes there'd be stupid people who were scared of me because I'm different to others and they'd have no other way to deal with me

11

other than violence and hard words because they'd not know the secret of me.'

Mathew stopped and dropped his head and knew now that he'd said too much and that the priest would make him tell it all. But the priest said nothing, and after a while Mathew looked up and saw the priest watching him kindly.

'So anyway, Mathew. You'd heard the voices that night. What happened then?'

Mathew scrunched up his face and shut his eyes once more and thought back, further and further, till he had the night he wanted, and the silence of it, and the low murmur beyond in the street, and the sudden sound then like a child crying.

'There was another noise, Father, and I didn't know what it was. It was with the voices and it made me worry and I stood up as quiet as I could and slipped out of the sack and the coat and I crept along the fences the same way the voices and the noise were going, and I followed the sound of them till I came to Boat Lane and I crouched there in the darkness and waited for them to go by on the street, thinking maybe that I'd see the shape of them and know who they were.'

Mathew waited for a moment to catch his breath and to take a look at the priest's face. The priest was watching him still, still kindly, and he smiled now, as if to encourage. Outside, the sky was darkening again, another shower coming.

'I got an awful fright, Father, because they stopped at the end of the lane and I thought for a moment that they'd seen me or heard me, but they hadn't because they made no move towards me. There was two of them. Two grown men, and at first I could not tell who they were. They had stopped talking, and they did not move, and they looked up the lane to where I was and my heart stopped beating in case they'd hear it. There was a shape between them, that one of them clutched, and I saw after a while that the shape was a child, because it had legs but it was small, only coming up to the men's middles. It made little noises, Father, frightened noises, and it wriggled like it was tied.'

'My God, Mathew. Why have you told no one?'

'Because of what happened, Father,' said Mathew, and then thought for a moment about what it was he meant and he wasn't sure that he knew. He became confused and started to talk again before he was ready and a babble of sounds came out of him and a small belch too and he went red and fell silent, and heard the rain hit the window. The priest sighed and ran his hand over his head.

'Go on then, Mathew. What happened?'

'One of the men, Father, he spoke. He said, "He's late", and the other grunted and they stood looking up the lane. I knew them then. I knew them by the voice of the one who spoke, and by the way they were waiting like that, the two of them, on a third.'

'McCauley,' said the priest suddenly, and Mathew jumped. 'McCauley and Brennan and that other one, what's his name?'

'Peter Higgins, Father. They call him Hog.'

'Hog. That's it. My God. That crowd. What on earth were they up to?'

Mathew smiled and looked at the priest, at his flushed face and his big nose. He was not a lovely man like Garda Cullen had been, but he was kind in the same way, and friendly, and he spoke to him like a sensible person, not like he was rushing and hard to understand.

'Go on, Mathew, please.'

'Well, Father, I know Bat Brennan and Hog, and they know me, and I don't like them much, but they're big and slow and stupid, forgive me, Father, but they are, and I'd keep out of their way but I'm not scared of them. Mr McCauley though, he's different. He's quiet and he has dead eyes and I saw him once snap the neck of a bird for no reason I could see at all.'

'No, he's a dark man.'

'He is, Father, so I was scared there where I was and I didn't move. If it had been only Bat Brennan and Hog then I would have been brave, Father, and went to them asking what it was they thought they were doing with a child tied between them at the dead of night by Boat Lane. I would have, Father. But I knew it was Mr McCauley they were waiting on, and all my braveness left me, Father, I'm sorry.'

The priest nodded and made a shape with his lips and the rain kept on at the window. It was cold now and Mathew shivered a little but the priest did not notice.

'Did you stay put, Mathew?'

'I did, Father. I stayed put. Once or twice they said something to each other and Bat Brennan shook the child one time, and told him to shut up.'

'It was a boy, then.'

'I didn't know it then, Father, but, yes, it was a little boy, little Michael Brennan.'

'Brennan's son?'

'Yes, Father.'

'What on earth? I saw him yesterday, playing. He's fine.'

'Oh he is, Father, yes. Fine and fit.'

The priest looked at Mathew uncertainly. 'Well, you'd better go on then, Mathew. Tell me what happened.'

His voice had changed and Mathew felt a little sad all of a sudden, and even colder, because he knew that the priest did not believe him any more, that he thought it was a made-up story and that Mathew was having him on.

'Go on, Mathew.'

He would hurry him up now to get him to the end of it and then it would be out into the rain again for Mathew. He'd have to ask for his clothes back, and maybe the priest wouldn't want to give them to him, or would want the shirt and T-shirt and black pants back for them.

'Mathew?'

The rain was on at the window again like hail, a storm of it cluttering the view so that no sky could be seen at all, only the wash of the water. Mathew shivered. He would make a dash for the bit of a hut behind the school. It was nearest. He could stay there until the shower was over, and then maybe head out towards the lake and see what was up and it'd be time then to call at the convent for his tea, for the lovely white bread, and the gravy on the potatoes, and the chop and the sprouts all mixing up in his mouth like he was the king of Ireland at his feast with the day's hunting done.

'Maffew? Moth's gone?'

What was he on about now, the priest? Moth? What moth? He was making no sense now. It was time to go now. Out into the rain.

It was a thing about the rain. Having to go into it from a dry place, that was harder than being in it all the time.

Fr Devoy watched Mathew Doyle scamper through the downpour and disappear behind the schoolhouse, carrying his filthy jeans in one hand and the bag of fruit and chocolate that he'd been given in the other. He ran at a lopsided gait, more like a monkey than a man. He had insisted on taking the jeans despite Fr Devoy's offer to have them washed. He'd become incoherent by then though, babbling away about kings and nuns and apparently unable to understand much of what was said to him.

15

Fr Devoy closed the door and went back to the kitchen where he made himself another cup of tea and lit a cigarette and watched the rain. It was curious. It had been the first time that he had had any kind of intelligible conversation with Mathew Doyle since arriving in the parish nearly a year before. At first the man had run from every approach, and Fr Devoy had been upset at that. But Dr Brooks had had a word with him, telling him much of Mathew's story, and advising the adoption of a more gentle, unobtrusive, almost disinterested aspect, which, he assured the priest, would be more likely to generate trust. So, instead of trying to talk to the fellow, Fr Devoy had merely smiled and nodded until eventually Mathew began to nod back, and then to smile, and after some months to blubber some class of a greeting which took a little interpreting but seemed to be, 'Hello, Father, God bless your feet.'

But what of his story? What was he to make of that? He saw no reason for the poor creature to lie. But his imagination was a child's imagination, an unruly thing that stretched itself through all of his behaviour, removing, or at least obscuring, his reason, and making him what he was – unsuited for the world. Fr Devoy had come across him once talking animatedly to a gable wall. Lucidly too. He seemed to be arguing with the stone on some point of history. 'It was a good century for the church,' he had been saying, 'but not a good one for God', before swinging on his heel to find Fr Devoy there. He had blubbered and fled, and Fr Devoy had for the first time felt the sadness that all the town seemed to share when it came to the subject of Mathew Doyle. There was a good mind in there somewhere. A very good mind. The town knew it, and was sad because of it, and protective too. Protective and proud.

'It may be said of this town, Fr Devoy,' Grealy the shop-

16

keeper had told him, 'as of no other town in Ireland, that our village idiot is a genius.'

The civil spirit was not shared, Fr Devoy had no doubt, by Mr Brian McCauley, a farmer originally from the north, who moved through the small streets like a dark cloud, bitter and vindictive. He was born a Protestant, they said of him, and had converted as a young man to marry a Catholic girl from Downpatrick. The odium of his family and hers had driven them south, sacrificing their birthright for love, and for a small piece of poor pasture on the foothills of the Dublin mountains left to the girl by a sympathetic uncle. McCauley lived there now alone, his wife dead from a young age, leaving him childless and bitter in a place where he was not at home.

Fr Devoy had visited him once, a month or so after arriving, unaware of his character. He had left his farm convinced that if there was ever a man unwilling to feel the warmth of Christian compassion and neighbourliness, and determined to make of his life the hard ground of which Our Lord spoke, then it was this man. He was set against goodness as others are set against evil.

But what interest would he have in arson? What possible good could it do him to burn down the cinema, and Gill's butchers and Dr Brooks's stables? There was no sense to it. Although only the cinema had been definitely confirmed as arson, and Mathew Doyle had spoken only of it, not of the others. But there was little doubt, in Fr Devoy's mind, or in the minds of everyone else, that all three had been deliberately set. Helen Brooks's outburst towards Mathew could, Fr Devoy supposed, be put down to grief at the loss of her horses, and the small whispers that were doing the rounds, as always in situations like this, blaming the strangest member of the community for the community's misfortunes.

Mathew Doyle was strange indeed, but incapable of doing such a thing. Fr Devoy was sure of that, and he had been there only a year. Dr Brooks would know it too, better than anyone, as would his daughter. But Helen was capricious; a pampered and volatile girl. She might well train her anger on the easiest target.

But McCauley? And with Bat Brennan bringing his child, tied between him and Hog Higgins as though kidnapped. Why? Fr Devoy rubbed his eyes and lit another cigarette and looked out at the rain. Mathew Doyle had not told him enough. How long it might be before he was once again sufficiently lucid to finish the tale, Fr Devoy could only imagine.

The rain was stopping, he thought. But after this shower was another, and another after that, like flocks of birds passing over the town, the flapping of their wings sending a chill through the air.

Helen cut her hand on a charred timber and looked at the blood that appeared through the ashes and cried for the first time. Her jeans were filthy now, with mud and rain and the blackness of the stables. Her hair fell over her eyes in wet ropes and she felt a pain in her heart, or where she thought her heart might be, or where it had been, for it was gone now, dead, smoke against the sky, with Poppy and Gepetto and Mountain Star.

She cried great sobs and made strange noises and did things with her hands that she could not understand. Then she realized that she had not cried like this before, ever, not even when her mother had died, and that made her cry all the more, appalled that her grief was greater for her horses than it had been for Mam. Mam. She remembered her mother's soft voice and wanted to hear it, and to have

18

her hold her and cuddle her and stroke her hair and whisper to her that it was all right, that morning would come and then the world would start again.

They had kept her from the fire. She had stood in her nightgown, sweating from the heat of the flames, fighting against the arms of Mrs Hartigan that held her, confused by the brightness that was brighter than the day, while from somewhere so close that she could hear their hearts beating, her three horses screamed and pounded their hooves and screamed again, and her father, his pyjamas turning black, and Dan Hartigan and Garda Sweeny and the rich man from the big house, all ran about the yard with tiny buckets, dropping water on the cobbles and crying in frustration, and struggling then to stretch a hose from the shed, and her father bellowing out of him the worst of curses as they watched the pathetic trickle of it swallowed by the fire as if the water had forgotten what it was, and Dan Hartigan and the rich man holding back her father, and Garda Sweeny standing as if his shoulders had been snapped, and all the time the screaming and then worse than the screaming, the stopping of the screaming, and the silence that followed it, broken only by the soft thunder of the fire and the splintering of wood and the sound of air being sucked in, until Helen fell limp in Mrs Hartigan's arms and wished for herself the soul of a horse so that she could truly feel with them the roaring rush of dying.

The ashes were still warm.

She had been taken to the Hartigans' house, led away in a daze as the car, parked in the garage adjoining the stables, exploded behind her. They wrapped her in blankets and gave her tea. Mrs Hartigan told her that the fire brigade had come eventually, from Bray, and had put out the blaze, though it had lost much of its ferocity by then.

'Had it doused in minutes, they did. Such a shame they were no nearer. That's three times now that we might have been saved by having an engine of our own. But there's evil afoot, girl. Evil afoot.'

Her father had come for her in the morning, his hands blistered and his face red as if from the sun. They had walked home together and she had asked him about burying the horses, and he had muttered something about there being little to bury, and that it was already done, and she had nodded and was glad of it. She believed that horses were angels come to watch us, and that their bodies were hollow and their souls light. They were gone up now, into the sky.

The smell of the fire lingered like a bad meal and remained constant for days. Now, as she sat in the ashes and cried, it had become part of her, tangled in her hair and caught like dirt in the pores of her skin, and she was sure that she would never be rid of it. They would start to clear the mess tomorrow, her father and the Hartigans and Garda Sweeny. There had been no talk of new stables or new horses or of anything new at all. Her father had let her be. He knew her too well to try and comfort her. She would go to him when she was ready, and wrap herself in his big arms and let him rock her gently back and forth and kiss her hair and tell her that it would be all right, it would soon be morning, and the world would start again.

Fr Devoy knocked loudly on Dr Brooks's door and ran his hand over his warm scalp. He had carried his umbrella but had not had to use it. The sky was still black, and the air warm, and he suspected that there would be thunder before the night was done. For that reason he had walked rather than cycled, hoping for a lift home. It was only when he had reached the doctor's house and glimpsed the black shell of the stables through the trees at its side that he remembered that the car had been destroyed.

It was after nine now, a rectangle of day-bright sky in the west throwing the horizon into sharp relief, the line of the hills like shapes cut in black paper.

He heard footsteps inside and turned to face the door and adjusted his features to the sympathetic seriousness he felt was required. He had not talked to Dr Brooks since the fire.

It was Helen. She opened the door a crack and peered out and then opened it fully and stepped aside and nodded slightly and he could tell from her look that there would be no words from her if she could help it. She was tucked up inside herself like a child in a crib.

'Dear girl, how are you? But that's a fool of a question. I can only tell you how sorry I am. Deeply sorry. It has been an awful business.'

She nodded, and her mouth was set at such a strange curve that he thought for a moment that she might be sick. He stepped past her into the dark hallway and she closed the door.

'I've come to see your father, dear, if he's available.'

She nodded, waiting for him as he propped up his umbrella in the corner by the door and then took off his coat and hesitated, not knowing where to put it. She took it from him and threw it unceremoniously over the banisters next to two others, and Fr Devoy could not help thinking that a mother in the house would see to it that such things did not happen.

He followed her as she walked past the sitting room and the study, and the large portrait of her mother that hung, rather inappropriately Fr Devoy had always thought, directly opposite the entrance, welcoming every visitor with the

21

beauty of the dead woman, and her bright eyes, and the reminder that she was gone, and that this house was still, in many ways, a house in mourning. Fr Devoy had of course never met her. She had died a good five years before his arrival. But he had been left in no doubt that to a large extent she still dominated the house, and Dr Brooks. Whether for good or ill, Fr Devoy could not quite decide.

The doctor was in the big kitchen, sitting at one end of the long table, writing, his pipe in his mouth, a mug by his side, papers and books scattered all around. Behind him was the door that led to his surgery. A radio played classical music softly.

'Hugo,' said Fr Devoy gently.

Dr Brooks looked up, surprised, and pulled the pipe from the entanglement of his bushy beard and seemed to smile, though at this distance it was hard for Fr Devoy to tell. His beard lifted at the edges and his eyes widened. It may have been a smile.

'Hello, John, how are you?'

'I'm fine, thank you, Hugo. More to the point though, how are you?'

'Oh I'm all right. A little singed perhaps, a little frayed at the edges. But nothing serious. Come and sit by me. Have some tea.'

Helen had disappeared. Fr Devoy closed the kitchen door behind him and sat down facing the window.

'It's a hot night,' he said. 'There'll be thunder.'

Dr Brooks poured him a mug of tea.

'That's probably a little cool now, John. Do you want a hot drop?'

'A little cool is just what I want, Hugo.'

'We'll have a beer so, as soon as I've finished this. It's for the insurance people. They sent a man out today to look things over. Very cagey fellow. I think he believes I did it myself.'

'Oh I'm sure not.'

Dr Brooks sighed.

'Well, what of it,' he said, 'Let them think what they want. There'll be no money though until they get a police report, and even then it'll be a long time coming I shouldn't wonder. These damn forms are interminable.'

Fr Devoy nodded his head and sipped his tea and waited. He watched the sky move and thought he saw rain in the distance but could not be sure. Black clouds stretched their way down the slopes to the city, and lights could be made out on the outskirts and along the coast. They shimmered in the humid air and could not be trusted. They gave no clue of distance or boundary. On nights like this they seemed both pressed up close and safely remote, like the painted lights of a picture held up to the face. But they moved.

Fr Devoy had often stared down at Dublin and imagined it a pool that fills and empties, shrinks and grows. At times it was tiny and far off, a different world, a nightmare in his past. And at other times, and recently all the time, it seemed to follow him, and his memories were filled with it, and his eyes caught it, indistinctly, a movement in a dark place. And then it would become giant, a flood that reached upwards so that he could feel the damp and the swell of it, could foresee the mountains covered, the noise arrive, the restless violence of it swim over his new place and drown him. He fancied sometimes that the city had sneaked into their town at the dead of night and had started the fires, and had sneaked away again, watery and perverse.

'Oh damn it, John,' said Hugo Brooks suddenly, and Fr Devoy jumped. 'I'm not going to get through all this tonight. It can wait. They want bloody measurements. Can you credit it? They want me to measure something that isn't there any more.'

'Perhaps you have the plans?' said Fr Devoy.

'Yes, I probably do. I'll fish them out tomorrow.'

'The car is the priority. What will you get?'

'I have no idea. I'll have to get something soon. Kiely from Enniskerry is taking all my house calls. They won't want me back.'

'Get something German.'

Dr Brooks rubbed his eyes and pushed out his chest and made a loud bellowing noise.

'Forgive me John, I'm all tensed up. I could do with a hot bath.'

'Well, I won't keep you.'

'You can keep me as long as you like. I'm too tired for a hot bath and too angry to sleep. What I want is good company and some cold beer.'

He stood and went to the fridge, sucking on his pipe and flexing his shoulders. The radio played Tchaikovsky.

'I have Smithwicks only so it'll have to do you. I've not been near a shop in three days. Mrs Hartigan has kept us from starvation. Well, kept me in any case. I don't think Helen has eaten much.'

He handed Fr Devoy a cold can and a glass and sat down again.

'How is she?' asked the priest, pouring the beer and holding the empty can to his wrists then for the chill it brought.

'She's quiet. Her heart is broken.' He sipped his beer.

'I imagine,' said Fr Devoy, lighting a cigarette, 'that she's able to put it in perspective at least. A child who's lost her mother will be better able to see the loss of animals for what it is.'

Dr Brooks looked at him sharply.

'And what's that, Father?'

'A small matter, Hugo, in the scale of things.'

'Tell Helen that. Since her mother died those horses have been company and affection and constancy. She has been closer to them than any living creature.'

There was a small edge of anger in Dr Brooks's voice, but Fr Devoy was unable to tell at what or whom it was directed.

'Of course,' he said. 'Of course.'

They drank silently for a moment and Fr Devoy wondered whether the object of his visit – to tell Dr Brooks what Mathew Doyle had told him – was wise. He had no way of knowing how the doctor would react. He should first tell Garda Sweeny surely. But how could he be sure of the story without asking the man who knew Mathew Doyle best. And that was Dr Brooks.

'Here is the rain,' said the doctor, relighting his pipe.

And there was rain indeed, falling at first in huge drops that hit the window like a series of slow knocks, and coming faster then and smaller, until within only a few seconds there was a deluge.

'I saw Helen in the town today,' said Fr Devoy, as both men continued to stare out the window.

'Mmmm?'

'She was wandering really, I think, a little aimless. Then she saw Mathew Doyle and flew at him. You couldn't imagine that such a sweet girl would be capable of such rage. Poor Mathew fled like a frightened rabbit.'

Dr Brooks turned from the window and looked at him, surprised.

'What on earth did she say?'

'She accused him of lighting the fires, all of them, of being a murderer – I presume that's a reference to the horses – and of being, well, of being some kind of pervert.'

Dr Brooks arched his eyebrows and Fr Devoy pursed his lips and looked at the ceiling.

'What kind of pervert?'

'The solitary kind.'

Dr Brooks was still for a moment and laughed then, loudly, slapping the table. It was a strange sight, coming so unexpectedly, and Fr Devoy had to smile.

'Good God, John, you're such a Catholic. She called him a wanker?'

'And more Hugo. A lot more. I sincerely hope she doesn't get it from you.'

'And I hope she gets it from nowhere else. Wanker is her favourite at the moment though. She was roaring it at Gepetto only a few days ago when he refused a new fence and she went flying.'

'You don't encourage this, I hope?'

'I don't. Soulless Protestant though I am, John, I know how a young lady should behave. I think it's funny though, don't you? And it's no harm to know how it's done. She knows better than to accuse Mathew though. She really does. I'll have a word with her. Was Mathew upset?'

Fr Devoy drank from his beer and wiped his mouth. The rain was heavy still, and the gloom in the kitchen was thick and warm. The music could barely be heard above the noise from outside.

'No, I don't think so. A little confused perhaps. I went after him and we got caught in a shower and I took him home and gave him a change of clothes, and do you know, he talked to me, lucidly, intelligently, for half an hour or more.'

'Well, bravo, John. There's not many can boast that. You've won him over.'

'Perhaps. But it's what he said to me Hugo. It worried me greatly. Very distressing.'

He took his time and recalled to Dr Brooks, as best he could, the entire conversation. The rain did not relent and in the distance there were rolls of thunder. As he talked Fr Devoy felt beads of sweat form on his forehead. He wiped at them with his sleeve. By the time he had finished the darkness was so great that he could barely make out the shape of the doctor. There was just a smudge against the gloom, and the glow of the pipe.

'McCauley?' asked Dr Brooks, incredulously.

'McCauley.'

'But he didn't actually see McCauley?'

'No. At least, not that I know of. He became confused after telling me that the child was Brennan's own son. I lost him then. He wanted his jeans back and off he went.'

There was a crack of thunder, and a flash of lightning lit the room for an instant. Dr Brooks had his eyes closed.

'Can I turn on a light Hugo?'

'What? Oh, yes, of course. Was that lightning?'

'It was,' said Fr Devoy, snapping on the main light and flooding the room with a gentle brightness, much to his relief. Dr Brooks squinted for a moment and turned then to look through the window at the storm.

'We're in the thick of it,' he said. 'There's another.'

The lightning came first and there was a short pause this time before the thunder roared at them madly, causing the two men to stare at each other, a little wide-eyed, like startled boys.

'What is thunder, John?'

'I have no idea.'

The radio crackled in an ugly way and Dr Brooks switched it off.

'Is there no theology of thunder, then?' he asked. 'No papal bull on the matter?'

Fr Devoy smiled.

'There is not,' he said. 'Not that I am aware. And has your church not held a synod on it? Not taken a vote yet?'

'There is one planned I believe. Though there are fears that it will do the ecumenical cause no good.'

Another flash came, and repeated itself as if echoed, and a louder crash of thunder flew down at them, and Fr Devoy's smile left him.

'The Lord dislikes our tone, Hugo,' he said. 'And He will have noticed that it was you who set it.'

Dr Brooks laughed and stood up and walked to the kitchen door and called his daughter. There was no reply. He tried again, and returned then slowly to his seat and sipped his beer.

'I hope she's not out in this,' he said.

'She wouldn't be, would she?'

'She might. Her coat is still in the hall, so I assume she isn't. I don't want to go to her room and check. She is private with her grief.'

Dr Brooks set a match to his pipe once more though Fr Devoy was sure that it was not needed. There was silence for a moment, but for the rain. If it kept up much longer the south road would be flooded by the turn-off to O'Brien's farm, and he would get his feet wet on the way home.

'Mathew Doyle,' said the doctor, and had his words punctuated with a clap of thunder, 'has never told me a lie as far as I know. It's not his way. If anything I think perhaps his honesty is part of his problem. I don't think he would make something up.'

'He has a monstrous imagination though, Hugo.'

'You think so?'

'He plays like a child. He talks to walls. He has a toy soldier, apparently.'

Dr Brooks laughed. 'Oh John, what's monstrous in that? Yes, he has an imagination. It's well he does or he'd go mad.'

Fr Devoy raised an eyebrow. Mathew Doyle was mad already, surely?

'But that's with himself,' continued Dr Brooks. 'He has his own world. When he talks to others he moves into our world, as best he can. He copies our ways of talking, learns our language so to speak. And he tells the truth. He wouldn't know any other way. There's no self-interest in his dealings with others. I believe he finds us as weird and unsettling as we do him. Talking to us must be like talking to someone from another planet. Would you lie to someone from another planet?'

Fr Devoy had such difficulty grasping the notion at all that he could not answer.

'I believe what he says,' said Dr Brooks. 'No matter how odd. If he says that's the way it happened, then that's the way it happened.'

And again, the thunder stamped out a full stop to his words, so that Fr Devoy felt that there was no point in argument. He drank his beer.

'As to what it might mean,' the doctor went on, 'I have no idea. The thing would be for me to talk to him, get the rest of the story, and then go to the police, I suppose, and let them know.'

He scratched his beard and stared into space as more thunder rattled through the house and the lights flickered almost imperceptibly.

'I will find him tomorrow and . . .'

He was interrupted by a sudden loud banging at the front door, a persistent, desperate hammering that startled both men. They stared at each other, before Dr Brooks rose, and smiled.

'Well, well, Father John. Thunder and lightning and a pounding on the door. Isn't this the merry night?'

He left the room slowly and Fr Devoy followed him at some little distance, disliking the idea of being too far from the calm, burly figure. Joining the continuing noise from the front door there was suddenly the drumming of feet on the stairs. Over Dr Brooks's shoulder Fr Devoy saw Helen reach the hall and look at her father worriedly.

'It's all right, pet. I'll get it.'

She stood clutching the banister and watched her father, who paused at the door and peered through the small rectangle of stained glass in its centre as if it might be possible to see something there. Fr Devoy moved aside slightly, not knowing what to expect, but greatly alarmed by a sudden suspicion that it was Brian McCauley who was outside, armed with a canister of petrol and a box of matches. He glanced at Helen and saw the same fear on her face, though of course she would have no name for the arsonist.

Dr Brooks muttered something about a peephole, glanced at his frightened companions and seemed, Fr Devoy thought, to smile a little. He opened the door.

A black shape stood there, arm upraised in the action of knocking, the storm a flurry of rain and noise at his back, something held in his left hand. There was a second of silence before the shape seemed to fall forward across the threshold, brushing past Dr Brooks into the hallway, and clattering onto the stone floor with hard boots and gasps that might be heard from a dying man. He bent over, hands on his knees, and uttered a chaos of words that Fr Devoy could not arrange sensibly. Water fell from him as from a small cloud, and Fr Devoy marvelled at the sight, bewildered by the bizarre creature before him, and by the mingling that he felt within himself of fear and excitement. It was Garda Sweeny.

Dr Brooks closed the door on a sharp blast of thunder and there was a pause once more as the dripping policeman caught his breath and stood slowly upright.

'Take your time, Pat,' said Dr Brooks in a voice that seemed to Fr Devoy magnificently calm.

'It's Mathew, doctor,' gasped the poor man. 'Mathew Doyle. He's dead on the road.'

Helen had sat by her window and watched the tearing of the sky. She had opened the window and wet her hair with all the water of the world. She had thought she heard her father calling then, and had pulled her head back and dried her hair with a towel, and wondered whether you could be struck by lightning and swallow the power that had hit you and make it yours, so that your life would be electric and bright and burning to the touch. Her horses were dead and in the sky, and the sky whinnied and shook off water and kicked up sparks beneath its hooves.

'Gepetto,' she whispered.

'Poppy,' she whispered.

'Mountain Star,' she whispered.

And the sky reared up and flashed its teeth, and she could feel the power of it through the air, a wave of strength that drove into her and pushed her back upon her bed. She lay there and closed her eyes, and was like a river that is swum by horses, and she cried softly with the awful joy it gave her. For a long time she lay there. And then slowly, she stopped her crying, and sat up, surprised, and noticed a change in herself that at first she did not understand.

31

Her mind was filled with a calm brought by the storm. It was as if the world now was racked with her grief, as if the skies cried her tears for her, the heavens took over her wailing, her roars, her moans, as if the air shot itself through with the shocks that would otherwise have cracked her bones and scarred her soul.

She stood and went to the window and looked out at the night. It raged. She was still. It was as though she had been released for a while, and was free to wander, sane, through the landscape of her madness. She wanted suddenly to be out in it, to walk through the fields and the lanes and the places where her horses had galloped and walked, jumped and sang. The places she had lived most.

Then came the knocking, the pounding, the hammering – like a finger of thunder come to tap at their door. Helen was not startled. She considered the sound, and heard the panic in it, and rose slowly and left her room. At the top of the stairs she heard her father and Fr Devoy come from the kitchen and tried to beat them to it. But her father said something to her and peered through the glass and muttered to himself and made her a little angry, and she made a face that Fr Devoy caught. He seemed too frightened though to notice.

When Garda Sweeny tumbled through like a fish plucked from the river, and flapped about for a moment, Helen thought suddenly that there had been another fire, and felt her anger grow inside her and fill her almost to bursting. But when he said instead that it was Mathew Doyle, and that he was dead, she felt nothing. Shock perhaps. Then confusion.

'There's blood all over him, doctor,' Garda Sweeny was gasping. 'The back of his head all matted with it and mangled and him lying there like a felled tree face down in the road, and there's a big steel bar beside him, so he's not only dead but murdered too. Hello, Father.'

'Dear Lord,' said the priest, blessing himself.

'Did you feel for a pulse?' asked Dr Brooks, and Helen saw a little doubt creep into the policeman's eyes.

'No I didn't, doctor. I'll grant you that. But he's not moving, nor is there a sound out of him, and to tell you the truth, you'd be afeared out there on a night like this, dark as the grave and the storm howling and me with only a ratty cape and a flashlight that couldn't pick out an arse in a pair of trousers. Sorry, Father. Oh, Miss Helen, beg your pardon, didn't see you there.'

As the man babbled, her father motioned to her and she understood and went through the kitchen to the surgery and got his bag. On her way back she saw the beer glasses on the kitchen table. Without thinking she drank what was left in both of them. She prayed to the spirits of her horses that her stupid shouting at Mathew that afternoon in the street had not been overheard by some other injured party. Mathew had not lit the fires, she knew that. She had been provoked by the stupid look on his face when she'd seen him, like a man who was still a child, or a child who wears a grotesque, adult mask, all yellow teeth and leathery skin, and his chest like the chest of a boy she would like to be with, and his eyes like a horse's eyes.

On her way back out to the hall she bumped into Fr Devoy who seemed to be moving back and forth for no reason.

'My umbrella?' he asked her.

'There,' she said and pointed.

Garda Sweeny was sitting on the stairs and her father throwing questions at him still.

'Did you move him?'

'No.'

'Did you touch him?'

'Sort of shook his shoulder.'

'Was he wearing a shirt?'

'No. Mathew? No.'

'Was his skin cold or warm?'

'Everything's warm tonight, doctor.'

Helen took her father's coat and hat from the banisters. Her father put them on and took his bag and nodded at her.

'You stay here, pet. Open up the surgery and prepare some bandages and disinfectant. And ring an ambulance, though they might not get through this.'

As he spoke the thunder rolled once more.

'And ring the station, too, please Miss,' said Garda Sweeny, 'and get them to get in touch with Miller in Bray, and tell them to send everyone out here except Danny Boylan, who can hold the fort.'

'Are we right then, gentlemen?' asked the doctor.

'I pray I'm not needed,' said Fr Devoy. Helen nodded.

She opened the door for them and they set off, Garda Sweeny first, trotting ahead, motioning, his feeble torch pointing in front of him, illuminating nothing but the rain. Her father followed, his big shape getting smaller, and Fr Devoy brought up the rear, controlling his umbrella with difficulty, scurrying after the others like a man chased by a dog.

Helen watched them, and let the rain catch her and the thunder shake her and the lightning light her. She stared at the black sky and tried to pray, but felt instead that she was prayed to, beseeched, implored by the heavens to be strong in these hours. There would be a battle. There would be a rage poured through her. The god of horses and of good men had a use for her.

She promised to be ready.

*

'Here doctor, here, mind the ditch,' called Garda Sweeny.

'I see him,' shouted Fr Devoy, his eyes on a strange shape at the side of the road, pelted by the rain.

'Get the torch here,' boomed the voice of Dr Brooks.

'It's near dead.'

'Holy God. Our Father who art in heaven . . .'

'Is he gone, doctor?'

'Give me your cape. Shine the torch on my bag.'

'. . . thy kingdom come, thy will be done . . .'

'Is he breathing, doctor?'

'Hold that there.'

'Take the torch, Father.'

'. . . give us this day our daily bread . . .'

'Oh the blood!'

'Hold it tight, man, tight.'

'. . . as we forgive those who trespass against us . . .'

'Turn him over. Gently now.'

'How can he be skinny and heavy?'

'Mathew?'

'. . . but deliver us from evil, Amen.'

Fr Devoy had thrown aside his umbrella and he held now the dying torch, its dim beam throwing an eerie pale glow on the face of Mathew Doyle. The wound was at the back of the head and there was much blood still, despite the rain. Garda Sweeny held a padded bandage to the place while Dr Brooks felt Mathew's head and neck. There must be nothing broken then, thought Fr Devoy, or the doctor would not have turned him over. Unless . . .

'He's alive all right,' said Dr Brooks.

'Oh, thank God.'

'Is he?'

'Mathew?'

There was blood from his nose, and a cut above his eye.

35

Fr Devoy felt something beneath his foot. It was an iron bar, like a bar from a gate.

'Mathew? Can you hear me son? It's Hugo. Can you hear me?'

There was thunder, and a flash of lightning, and the torch coughed a little brightness and died. Then a horrible, hellish moan came from the wounded man, and Fr Devoy shuddered and Garda Sweeny cursed.

'We have to move him,' said Dr Brooks. 'He's half frozen here. We have to get him back to the surgery.'

In the darkness they struggled with the dead weight and eventually, with Dr Brooks holding his shoulders, Garda Sweeny supporting his head and Fr Devoy carrying his feet, they began to make progress.

'Wait,' called the policeman.

'What is it?'

'The bar.'

'The what?'

'The weapon. The murder weapon. I have to get it.'

Garda Sweeny had stopped in his tracks.

'We don't have time,' the doctor told him.

'I'm sorry, doctor, but it's my duty to retrieve the murder weapon.'

'Please don't call it the murder weapon,' said Fr Devoy. 'Mathew's alive.'

'Beg your pardon, Father. The attempted murder weapon.'

'For God's sake,' roared Dr Brooks. 'If you waste any more bloody time then it will be the murder weapon. And I just might make it the double murder weapon. Now get moving before this man bleeds to death.'

And his words once more were followed by a crash of thunder as if God's fist pounded God's table in agreement, and Fr Devoy wondered how the doctor did it. They moved on.

The telephone was dead. Helen held it to her ear for a long moment and could hear nothing. She checked the lead, made sure that it was still connected to the wall. It was. She ran upstairs to her father's room and switched on the light and checked the telephone there, but it too was dead. On the floor by the bed she saw her mother's slippers. She gasped at them, stalled.

The lights went out.

She stood still, stone still. There was a silence. Then the rain came hard against the window and the thunder roared as loud as ever and the room was lit for a second by a bluish flash as if God was taking photographs. Her mother's dressing gown was laid out on the bed, a flower of some kind where the head should be. In the darkness then Helen was for a moment frightened, thinking that there must be someone in the house, someone who knew her mother's clothes, who knew where to find them, someone who had cut off the telephone and the electricity, someone who watched her through the door that she was sure had been open wider than it was now.

She sat on the bed and clutched her temples and rocked a little back and forth. There was no one. At night she had heard her father talking, had crept out to the landing and listened at his door. He talked in an ordinary voice, not a whisper, and he told his dead wife what he had done that day. Sometimes he laughed. Sometimes he asked her something, and there would be a long silence then and she would hear him gently sobbing and she would creep back to bed. She had seen him once or twice bringing flowers to his room, cheerfully, his big shoulders soft with happiness.

The telephone and the electricity had been knocked out by the storm.

She stood and walked calmly out of the room, and downstairs. In the cupboard in the hall she found a bag of candles and she set about lighting and distributing them in the hall and the kitchen. She kept most of them though for the surgery, which she now unlocked and entered, almost tripping over her father's chair. She placed two candles on the desk and another three on top of filing cabinets, and another one on the small shelf above the sink. She could see no way of lighting the bed where her father would place poor Mathew. There was a glass cabinet by its foot which reached all the way to the ceiling, and for which she had no key.

She opened a large drawer at the base of the desk and removed various bandages and swabs and a bottle of disinfectant. Before she could do anything more she heard a distant knocking at the front door. She paused, unsure. There was some thunder, and then the knocking came again, louder. She raced through the kitchen and the hall and the small flames of the candles danced in her wake and sent up strange strings of thin smoke like circus tricks. She threw open the door and admitted the wind and the rain, and the three soaked figures with their miserable burden.

'The electricity is gone?' her father gasped.

'Yes. And the telephone.'

'Dear God,' spluttered Fr Devoy.

'No stopping here. On to the surgery. Is it opened?'

Helen nodded and went ahead of them, clearing what she could clear from their way. She looked at Mathew and saw blood on his face, and his eyes now closed, now open, rolling back in his head, his skin as white as paper, spittle on his chin and his mouth open and his teeth black and his chest like the chest of a boy, the policeman's cape as black against it as coal against snow. Mathew moaned loudly and Helen shuddered.

'On the bed, gently now.'

The three men manoeuvred with difficulty, and with much grunting and groaning until eventually Mathew was laid gently onto the plastic mattress, his head still held by Garda Sweeny.

'Don't let go, but don't hold it at too much of an angle. That's it.'

Helen watched her father, his brow dripping with rain and sweat, as he took off his coat and washed his hands and rummaged amongst bottles and looked at what she had put out for him.

'Thanks, pet. Heat some water for me, will you?'

'There's no electricity.'

'There's a small gas stove under the sink. See if you can get that going. But first bring me some ice and a jug of water. All right? And get these coats out of here.'

In the kitchen as she worked she could hear the moans of the wounded man, and the steady voice of her father issuing instructions, and the mumbling of the priest and the policeman. She brought in the ice and the water, and gasped a little at the bloody swabs and bandages discarded in the metal bucket.

'Mathew?' said the priest. 'Mathew, lad, can you hear me?'

Mathew's eyes were open and he was staring about him, terrified.

'Mathew?' said the doctor. 'Mathew, it's all right, it's Hugo. Don't worry. You're in my house. You've had a nasty blow on your head. We'll fix you up in no time. You relax. Is it painful?'

Mathew groaned and closed his eyes and Helen's father

39

sighed as if relieved and resumed snipping at the hair around the wound with small silver scissors.

'Did you find the stove, pet?'

'No. I'll get it now.'

She suspected that she was being kept out of the way, and knew as soon as she had thought it that it was not the case. He would need hot water to clean the wound before he applied stitches. But she could not help thinking that it was the priest who should see to it. He was standing there mumbling his prayers, his bald head sweating, and his hands trembling. Or the policeman, who sat now in her father's chair, breathing heavily, dripping onto the desk, a slight leathery smell from him, like a saddle smell. Helen wanted to work with her father, and most of all she wanted to hear whatever Mathew had to say.

She found the stove and after a few moments managed to light it, the blue flame rising suddenly with a pop. She filled a pot with water and balanced it on the thin metal arms over the heat. She moved nearer the surgery door and listened.

'Is it bad?' the priest was asking.

'It's a long cut, but not that deep. It looks like he was moving away from it. Head wounds always produce a lot of blood. There's no obvious fracture. I'll have to get him X-rayed for a hairline. There's no neck injury either. All in all he's lucky. Concussion certainly, and his head will hurt like hell for a while, but he's lucky.'

'Well, thank God.'

'Was it meant to kill him though, doctor?' asked the policeman.

'I wouldn't know that.'

'Dear God,' said the priest.

There was a silence and Helen checked the water.

'... thinking what I'm thinking,' her father was saying.

'That we were overheard?' said Fr Devoy.

'Who?' asked Garda Sweeny.

'Mathew and myself.'

'Saying what?'

Suddenly there was a string of sounds from Mathew that made Helen jump. She could make out no individual words, only the terror in the voice, and a kind of pleading that frightened her.

'It's all right, son,' said her father gently. 'It's all right. No one's going to hurt you. You're quite safe here.'

'Sneaking,' said Mathew clearly. 'I'm sneaking as a cat.'

'What's he saying?' asked Garda Sweeny in a whisper, as if it was a ghost talking, or an apparition.

'Lights in the sky,' Mathew continued. 'Sneaking, nothing, oh dear, oh dear, bastard I bastard. His eyes. Pain in us. Starting like a flower and then like a gas in the chamber of the head.'

'Ssh, Mathew. It's all right. Be still.'

'Pain in us. Smothering and burning. All the dead horses and all the dead men.'

There was a hissing behind Helen. She turned and saw the water boiling. She ran and switched off the stove and topped up the pot with cold water from the tap and carried it through to the surgery. Mathew was sitting up. He looked at her.

'Horses,' he said, and his face, bloody and stretched with pain, was the saddest face she had ever seen.

'I'm sorry,' she said. 'I'm sorry I shouted at you.'

He looked at her for a moment longer, and she wasn't sure whether he had understood. Then he closed his eyes and lay back and moaned.

'Listen to me now, Mathew,' said Garda Sweeny, getting

41

up from the chair and moving towards the bed. 'It's very important now that you tell me what happened. Who hit you? Mathew?'

But Mathew lay still and kept his eyes closed and the only sound he made was a kind of humming, like the humming of a small engine, constant and mild and determined.

'Perhaps you gentlemen could wait in the kitchen while I wash and dress Mathew's head,' said Dr Brooks, and Helen smiled. 'Helen, you can act as nurse, please.'

Garda Sweeny frowned and hesitated, but Fr Devoy immediately shuffled out, still breathing heavily, his bald head damp, his eyes darting, frightened.

'If he starts to talk, doctor, you'll call me,' said the policeman. Dr Brooks nodded and Sweeny looked again at Mathew and frowned. He sighed slightly, officiously, and left the room, tugging sharply at his tunic. Mathew lay still, and hummed like the dream of a sleeping child hums above the child's head.

'Now Helen, pet, the water, and some more swabs, please.'

She helped her father and got blood on her hands, and she held Mathew and stroked his shoulder and mopped his brow and whispered softly to him as he groaned and winced with pain. His eyes opened rarely and he hummed when he was not groaning, at a pitch that struck her, and she did not know why, as having something to do with the storm, in harmony with the thunder and the pelt of the rain, and with the cracking of the lightning which she imagined Mathew felt in his teeth, such was the way he clenched them.

The storm was her heart and his dream. This was so.

Her father prepared an injection while she lay a damp cloth over Mathew's forehead and found his coarse, big hand and held it. He tensed with the needle, and the humming paused and the thunder also, and for a moment she was tired, but then he relaxed once more and the thunder cracked loudly and her jaw clenched and she felt the muscles in her body make themselves known to her as if they were answering a roll call, and remembered suddenly, and for no reason she could imagine, her mother showing her how to make gazpacho. Mathew squeezed her hand.

'Hold a candle for me, pet, while I stitch.'

Mathew hummed his way through the procedure and seemed to Helen immensely brave. And her father with his steady hands and the care he took, and the kind words he offered to his patient for reassurance, seemed to her to be the best of doctors, the gentlest, the most skilled, the ablest.

'Who's here, Hugo?' Mathew asked suddenly, leaving off the humming, or rather, Helen thought, swallowing it, tucking it away somewhere behind the bones of his chest, in amongst his fears and his strength.

'Just Helen and myself Mathew, just the three of us.'

'Miss Helen.'

'Yes, Mathew, I'm here.'

'Terror sorry for the horses. Terror sorry.'

'Thank you, Mathew. And I'm sorry for blaming you.'

'Yes. Horses.'

His eyes looked around him and stared bewildered at Garda Sweeny's cape that lay now across his middle.

'Is this mine?' he asked.

'No,' Helen answered. 'It's Garda Sweeny's.'

He turned his head to look at her and felt the tug of the thread and heard the doctor's sharp exclamation and froze, his eyes wide and frightened.

'What is it?' he gasped.

'It's all right Mathew, just stay still,' Dr Brooks said gently. 'You mustn't move until I'm finished.'

43

'Finished what?'

'I'm putting in a few stitches.'

Mathew kept looking at Helen, his face like a cartoon face, filled with fear and confusion.

'What's stitches?'

'Stitches like stitches in clothes.'

Mathew paused, and blinked once. 'Needle and thread stitches?'

'Yes.'

'Oh dear, Hugo. Oh dear. Don't do that. That's all right. Don't do that, I'm not torn, I'm only bumped. Just a couple of tablets for my headache and it'll be all all right. Don't go darning me like a sock. I'm not a sock.'

'No, Mathew, I know . . .'

'I've not a hole in me, I don't need a needle and thread, just a tablet and a nice drink Hugo, oh dear, I'm not , . .'

'Shut up, Mathew,' said Dr Brooks, quite crossly, and Mathew made a face as if a great curse had been uttered, and half smiled then, as a child might smile at a bad word, and made Helen laugh.

'It's almost finished,' Dr Brooks said. 'I know you're not a sock, and you won't feel a thing. So be still now and let me get on with it.'

'Yes, Hugo.'

'Good man.'

The thunder rattled the bottles in the cabinet, and the lightning could be seen through the small frosted windows high in the gable wall, and the candles seemed to draw back their light for a moment; and in this brief hesitation, where the gloom was deeper and the air more chill, Mathew said: 'It was Mr McCauley hit me.'

Helen did not understand the words for a moment. Then she glanced at her father, who concentrated on his task and made a small, encouraging, inquisitive noise that Helen thought bad acting.

'He was waiting for me as I came from the convent after my tea and I was late because Sister. Sister. Sister.'

He scrunched his eyes shut. 'Sister Gerard told me a long story about a woman in Dublin who dreamed the whole future of the world until the time when Our Lord comes back and points and dances and the end of the world happens then like a film ending.'

He opened his eyes and licked his lips. 'It was a good story but it was hard to know if it was true because everything the woman dreamed was in the future, which is things that have not happened yet, and she might have made it all up and fooled Sister Gerard completely. But it made me late and when I passed the lane to Mr McCauley's farm he was standing there with a big metal stick and he shouted and chased me and screamed at me that I was not to tell anybody that it was him I saw setting fire to the cinema or he would kill me and then he killed me anyway. Or that's what I thought.'

He sighed and shook his head.

'Ah, ah,' said Dr Brooks sharply.

'Oh, sorry, Hugo.'

'That's all right. I'm on the last one.'

Mathew touched his fingers to the cut above his eye and looked at the small amount of blood that clung to them.

'It's hard to die,' he said quietly, 'because it hurts in the part of the head where you've been murdered, but it's not as hard as you might think because there's singing and warmth and a great view. You can see the whole country from death, and the sea as well, and all the people you ever knew. They flit past you like when you're in a car and you have your head set sideways and fixed and you see lamp posts go by one after the other until you come to town, but it's different to that because when you see the lamp posts, then once you've passed them they're gone and you've lost them and you can't see them again, but in death it's different, it's like you collect the lamp posts and carry them with you, but of course they're not lamp posts at all but all the people you've ever known who were good to you. I saw yourself, Hugo, and Miss Helen too, and Fr Devoy and Mr Grealy and the Gill brothers and Mr and Mrs Hartigan and Sister Gerard and then I thought I was seeing things because there was Mrs Murtagh and Garda Cullen and them both dead these years and then I saw . . .'

And here Mathew spoke almost in a whisper and looked at Helen, and she could see tears in his eyes. 'I saw Mrs Brooks, your lovely mother, and she was standing there as beautiful as the morning, and she smiled at me and waved, and said something that I couldn't hear, and by her shoulder with their heads in brightness were Poppy and Gepetto and Mountain Star. The horses reared up and whinnied and I could hear that, and I could feel the damp breath of them on my neck and I could feel how strong they were and they nuzzled me and whispered horse secrets that I can't remember, about how the world was made and how it moves, and then suddenly everything went black and the pain came once more and I opened my eyes and saw your father looking at me. Then I fell asleep. Then I woke up and there was a storm and I was flying through it on my back and then I fell asleep and then I woke up and I was here and I was awful sore and your father sewing me up like a sock and that's where I am now, before I started to tell you . . . what I'm telling you.'

He paused and considered her. Helen looked into his eyes.

'Did you ask me something in particular?' he said. 'Or am I making conversation just?'

Helen could not answer. She shook her head and felt her heart press against her insides and her eyes fill with salt water.

'All done,' said her father softly. 'All finished.'

They lay Mathew back on some pillows and cleaned the small cuts on his face and applied plasters. He kept his eyes shut and resumed his humming. Helen took two blankets from the box beneath the bed and laid them over him. He sighed. Then she filled a glass from the tap and put it in his hand.

'Thank you, Miss.'

'Take these, Mathew,' said the doctor. 'Put them on the back of your tongue and then take a gulp of water and swallow them. They'll help your headache and you can have a wee sleep. All right?'

Mathew nodded and did as he was told, spilling some water but getting the tablets down.

'He must have heard me,' he said as he lay down again. 'He must have heard me telling Fr Devoy about what happened the night of the fire at the cinema. But I didn't tell Fr Devoy everything. I just told him the start.'

'Will you tell me the rest?' asked the doctor.

'What if he hears?'

'He won't. He's not anywhere near here. And I'm with you anyway and I won't let you out of my sight. Tell me what happened.'

Helen stepped back a little, towards the door, into the shadows. Mathew closed his eyes and was silent for a moment.

'I was asleep behind Grealy's.'

'Tell me from the place where you're hidden in Boat Lane

47

and you can see Higgins and Brennan and the boy tied between them.'

Helen was not surprised. As soon as she had heard the name of McCauley she had in her own mind named Brennan and Higgins as well. The three were one. But a boy? Tied?

'That was little Michael, Hugo. He was tied at his wrists and they had a rag around his mouth so he wouldn't be noisy. I was awful frightened Hugo, because I knew who it was they'd be waiting for. It was bound to be Mr McCauley. And after a few minutes didn't he appear at the other end of the lane and I nearly died right there because I knew he'd have to walk past me to get to them and I made myself as small as I could by breathing in and thinking of a mouse.'

He demonstrated, hissing in a long breath and curling up his legs and folding his arms around his torso. It seemed to Helen that he did become very small, though by the look on his face it was an uncomfortable exercise.

'That's all right, Mathew. Relax now.'

'I'd do it better Hugo but my head is not my own. It's throbbing and as big as Fr Devoy's head.'

Helen smiled, as did her father.

'Go on anyway, Mathew.'

'Well Hugo, Mr McCauley was there, and I swear that I felt him before I saw him. He came fast through the lane and then stopped. Right beside me. I closed my eyes and waited to be murdered, because I was sure that I would be. As close to me as you are. I could have touched the long coat on him.'

He broke off and turned to the doctor. 'Puce means the colour of a flea, did you know that, Hugo?'

'I didn't, Mathew, no.'

'Well, I'm sure that I was the colour of a flea because I was holding my breath so tightly that I was ready to burst open like a balloon. I thought if I didn't breathe I'd die, and that if I did I'd be murdered. So I opened one eye to see if I'd been seen because if I'd been seen then I might as well breathe as it would be as well to be murdered only and not murdered and suffocated too, if you know what I mean. I opened one eye and he was still as close to me as you are but he was motioning to the others to come to him up the lane, I suppose so as they wouldn't be seen on the street, and they were walking up the lane towards him and he standing as close to me as you are and me there drowning without a drop of water anywhere and by now half hoping that I'd be seen so that I would be able at least to take a breath before I died because my eyes were rolling back in my head like a dying dog's eyes. But they all came together and they didn't see me. They stood there and talked, Mr McCauley asking angrily who the child was and why was he there and Bat Brennan rushing out an answer so loudly that it allowed me to breathe out and the joy of that was wonderful and I was able to breathe a few times till I was breathing normally because of the noise that Bat Brennan made when he spoke, and when he tried to whisper it was only louder and I think it was mostly the fear of Mr McCauley that made him like that but anyway he told Mr McCauley that it was his son Michael that was with them and the reason that he was with them was that Mrs Brennan was staying with her sister and he was looking after Michael by himself and that the boy would not stay in the house because he was frightened of being on his own so that he'd had to take him with him and that they'd tied him because he was an awful nuisance and they'd gagged him because he had a habit of making noise when he shouldn't and Hog Higgins butted in then and said that it had been his idea to tie up the boy and Mr McCauley was quiet for a while and

he looked from one to the other and down at the boy
and back at them again and from one to the other and I was
waiting for my turn but it didn't come and I think he
was looking at them because he thought they were mad and
I was watching him so at first I didn't notice it but then I
did and I swear to God it was the most awful moment of
my whole life but there it was and I couldn't get away from
it but my eyes had met the big white eyes of little Michael
Brennan and him staring at me like you might stare at the
ghost of a man who's not dead yet. I think I must have
turned to stone. He stared at me and then he made a noise
beneath his gag, a hmm hmm hmm, as if he was trying to
tell them about me, and he lifted a foot and I thought he
was going to kick me but he was trying to point and just
then Mr McCauley dropped down and squatted in front of
him and looked him in the eyes and I thought he was going
to ask him, well, young man what is it you're trying to say
but he didn't instead he put a hand on his shoulder and told
him that his father was a stupid shite, excuse me, Hugo, but
he did, and that as far as he was concerned the boy wasn't
there so that any noise at all from him would be like noise
from a rat or a spider or a stray dog and those things that it
wouldn't give him a thought to kick to death, and he said
that if ever he talked about this night to anyone, ever men-
tioned it to anyone, even his mother, even his father who
was standing there beside him, then he'd be crushed like a
spider is crushed beneath the heel of a boot or like a dog is
crushed by a truck on the road and I think as he said it he
must have been squeezing the boy's shoulder very tight
because there was a look of pain in Michael's face, and he
winced a little and there was a trickling noise and a sob and
he'd wet himself and Mr McCauley said the name of our

Lord and stood up and clattered Bat Brennan across the side of the head and told him his son was a girl.'

Mathew paused for breath. His eyes were still closed. He gave a short sigh and continued. 'Well, he was so scared, the poor fellow, that I don't think he looked at me again, and I wouldn't be surprised if there was no memory in him of having seen me there at all.'

He paused again, and was silent for several moments.

'Go on, Mathew,' said the doctor gently.

'Oh dear,' said Mathew, opening his eyes suddenly and looking around. 'I dropped off there, Hugo, do you know? I'm awful sleepy and the pain in my head is not as bad.'

'That's the tablets I gave you. Finish the story anyway, Mathew, so you can go off to sleep.'

'I will. I will, Hugo,' said Mathew and closed his eyes again and pursed his lips. 'They moved off then, Mr McCauley shushing the others and small Michael Brennan walking strangely with his legs wide apart, and Hog Higgins laughing a little and Bat Brennan still whispering loud as anything to Mr McCauley about how sorry he was about Michael, but Mr McCauley telling him to shut up and then asking him if he had the petrol or would they have to use the child as a firelighter and Hog Higgins gave a great big guffaw at that but Mr McCauley gave him a dig and told him to shut up, and he did shut up then and didn't say another word again unless he was asked something by Mr McCauley. I heard the noise then of cans, of something being picked up, and it was the petrol they had in these big cans with handles on the tops and caps that you turn to open, and they made that sound that those things make when they hit against each other like the sound of big buckets of water, a kind of boing boing boing like an underwater sound, a whale sound, a sinking ships sound, a dungeon in the murky depths sound, a . . .'

'Yes, Mathew,' said the doctor. 'I know what you mean.'

'Well, I stood up very slow as soon as they were around the corner and I followed them and sneaked a look out onto the square and they were making their way around it close to the buildings towards the far side where the cinema is. Was. Where it was now but where it is then, Hugo, if you follow me.'

'Yes, go on.'

'And I crept around after them, far enough away so as not to be seen and if I was seen to get a good head start on them if they came after me, but not close enough to hear much of what they were saying any more. They stopped outside the cinema and Mr McCauley said something to the others and they looked at him and there was a silence, and then I heard him ask them loudly whether or not they were deaf, and they looked at each other and took their petrol cans and went over to the cinema and I couldn't see what it was they were doing really, but I caught a whiff of petrol, and then Mr McCauley did something awful strange, Hugo. He was standing there in the square in front of the cinema with the small boy tied and gagged beside him and them both looking at the others slopping around in the shadows and then suddenly he stretches his arms up over his head higher and higher until he's stretched out like a young tree in winter and he lets out of him this sort of low roar like an animal waking up and poor little Michael Brennan backs away from him some steps and falls down on his bottom and sits there looking up at Mr McCauley who's started now to shake and mutter and mutter and shake and shake and mutter and shake. "Annie," he calls. "Annie, oh Annie, oh Annie, oh," and then he pulls his fists in towards his chest and holds them there and the next thing I see is a small flame where he's lit a match but the way he's done it you'd think he'd pulled fire from his heart, and he walks slowly forward and Bat Brennan and Hog Higgins come scattering out of the shadows past him holding their heads, their petrol cans left behind them, scurrying away in two different directions, Bat Brennan almost forgetting his son, and turning then and picking him up and running as the big whumpf goes up behind them and pulls flames towards the heavens like a flower seen by a fly and pushing out an awful heat from it like a thousand heaters and everything melting in the air like butter, oily and blurred, and I had to close my eyes it was so bad and when I opened them I couldn't see Mr McCauley anywhere and I thought for a while that he'd been killed by himself but then the next day I saw him kicking through the wreck of it like all the other men did and I knew he wasn't killed, only touched in his head for his dead wife whose name was Anne and who died in 1965, in October it was, when the year is at its best, and her with the nicest smile I've ever seen. Ever seen at all.'

Helen watched her father and saw nothing of him move, just a slight flexing of his hands, a gentle folding in of his fingers, as he sat by Mathew's limp and narrow body, with its closed eyes and its shallow breathing. His head was slightly bowed, his elbows on his knees, and it was as if he waited at a deathbed for his grief to begin.

A candle hissed and went out. Helen looked at the tiny orange spark dying, and at the thin smoke that rose, coiling, and stopped rising then and disappeared against the gloom. She blinked, and lifted the candlestick and stepped quickly through the door and the small dim passage with its single candle, into the glittering kitchen, where the priest and the policeman sat huddled at the table like men from a different time.

'Is everything all right?' the priest asked, half rising.

'Yes.'

'Is he conscious?' asked the policeman.

'I don't know.'

'Did he say anything?'

'Yes.'

She put the candlestick down on the table and listened for the storm and could hear only the rain. The policeman walked past her towards the surgery.

'Are you all right?' the priest asked her, standing fully now, pushing back his chair noisily.

'Yes.'

'Can I get you anything?'

'No, thank you.'

She strained to hear thunder, but there was just the rain.

'I'll go and see Mathew, I think,' said the priest, moving slowly past her. 'They may need me there,' he mumbled.

Helen nodded. She thought she had heard distant thunder, but the priest had spoken over it. She walked quickly through the kitchen and into the hall, past a candle which spilled wax onto a table top and onto the floor, forming pearly stalactites like icicles. She glanced at the mess and thought of lightning, and grabbed her coat from the banister and opened the front door, afraid that there would be calm, a clear sky, a silence. But the rain was thick and the ground muddy, and a wind blew that was stronger than before, and as she shut the door behind her and moved down the driveway there were flashes in the distance and a rumbling that caught in her mind and reverberated, like the sound of a song. Her face and her hair became wet, and her coat sucked up the water like dry earth. She opened her mouth that she might taste the storm and was rewarded by a fork of lightning which found the ground somewhere in front of her, and a thunderbolt which left her ears ringing and her mind sharp and pointed like a sword.

She heard her horses in the sky, and felt the rage of her grief like a drug in her veins, pushing her blood, pushing her feet towards McCauley's, pushing her arms and her hands and her eyes and her blood, and her feet towards McCauley's.

Fr Devoy was terrified. It had taken hold of him on the road and he had not been able to shake it off, even in the tender candlelight of the kitchen where he waited with Garda Sweeny and heard the storm recede. The grip of the fear was somewhere above his stomach, in the tangle of places where his heart beat and his lungs worked. He felt out of breath, wide-eyed, tense, like a falling body waiting to hit the ground.

He could not name it. He thought at first, as they had carried the bloody weight back to the house, that it was a fear simply of violence, of being followed, attacked, of the pain that it would bring. But indoors then, safe from Brian McCauley, his agitation did not diminish. It remained constant, and he could not now imagine circumstances in which he might be rid of it, or return to even a semblance of calm. It was not the thunder and lightning, it could not be as minor as that. It might, he supposed, be shock, a kind of trauma of the senses, an assault on the stability of his feelings, even of his faith. For he felt powerless, as lost in the storm of all this as a child. He tried to pray and could only ramble, incoherent as a drunk, desperate, as if he had not prayed before, as if he had reached a last resort and had reverted to something remembered from childhood. Dear God, please save Mathew and stop the storm and bring back the electricity and the phones and get me out of here, thank you.

Sweeny fired questions at him about the conversation he'd had with Mathew, and which he now regretted intensely. The policeman badgered him, getting him to repeat some things which he jotted down in a notebook. When Fr Devoy had recounted all that he could recall, he watched Sweeny uneasily as he poked around the kitchen, flicking light switches and taking more than just a glance at the insurance forms which still lay on the table. He went out into the hall, and Fr Devoy could hear him trying the telephone and opening a door. As he walked back into the room he was writing again in his book.

'It's some house they have here, Father, isn't it?'

He didn't answer.

'The phone's still out.'

Sweeny finished writing, and put the book away and picked his nose.

'God, I'm soaked,' he said. 'I'll catch my death. Did you lose your umbrella, Father?'

'My what?'

'Your umbrella,' he said, opening an imaginary umbrella with a mime that looked somehow obscene.

'I left it on the road, where we found Mathew.'

Sweeny nodded and sat down, hitching up his trouser legs and running his hands along his thighs. 'God, I'm soaked.'

He looked towards the surgery.

'It's always the same,' he said. 'When there's someone you need to talk to, you're left waiting somewhere in a side room or a corridor, bored half to death, and when you're in need of a little peace and quiet you're being badgered from all sides by eejits.'

Fr Devoy smiled weakly.

'I wonder,' said the policeman, 'whether I should go out to the road and pick up the murder ... I mean the iron bar, the weapon, while I'm waiting. I could get your umbrella too.'

But he didn't move, he stayed seated at the table and began massaging his neck.

'If only I'd been on patrol when I found him,' said the policeman, 'and not on my way home. Then I'd have a car and a radio and a proper torch.'

What would it mean, thought Fr Devoy, if his faith was of no use to him here? What would it mean if he was close to God only in quiet times, in the still of the church, on his knees in his room, alone on the roads and in the fields, walking in the sunshine and the mild air? What would that mean? For the first time since his trouble in Dublin he was cut adrift from the everyday, he was thrown into something else, and once more, God was not following.

He closed his eyes and tried to focus on the third sorrowful mystery, the crowning with thorns. Moral courage. He pictured the Lord, on his knees, his arms bound, his head bowed, his silence. The soldiers, how would they grip the crown without pricking themselves? They would have to leave a section thornless. And the soldier who weaved this crown, had he worn gloves? If he had not then he too had suffered. His hands would be bloody, cut in the pads of the fingers, ripped in the palms.

'Is it brain surgery they're at in there?' asked Sweeny suddenly. 'Seeing if there is one perhaps.'

The Lord's silence. Why so much silence, after so much talk?

'Have you settled in then, Father?'

'What?'

'Have you settled in?'

'Where?'

'Here. In town.'

'Oh yes, of course. It's home now.'

'How long have you been here?'

'A little over a year now, I think.'

'Is it that long?'

Fr Devoy nodded. He did not like the policeman's tone. He knew exactly how long he'd been there. He sat every Sunday in the front of the church with his thin wife and his two children, his loud voice ringing out the responses.

'I didn't think it was that long.'

The Lord had felt the thorns resting on his head, and perhaps he had thought for a moment that it was not so bad. But then they had taken a club of some sort, or the flat of a sword perhaps, and had hammered those spikes into his flesh until his blood ran down over his forehead as it was portrayed in the paintings. And the blood would have run down the back of his head as well, to his neck and his shoulders. There was always a great deal of blood, Hugo had said, from head wounds.

'Pity we don't have a pack of cards,' said Sweeny with a laugh.

Fr Devoy smiled at him, feeling calmer. The Lord had suffered in silence, in strength, in humility. What was Sweeny's first name? Patrick. Pat.

'Will you pray with me, Pat?'

The policeman's mouth opened a fraction and he stared at Fr Devoy and smiled, and then stopped smiling.

'Pray?'

'Yes. We'll pray for Mathew, and for Brian McCauley too.'

'McCauley?'

'For him most of all.'

Sweeny's eyes narrowed and he considered Fr Devoy for a moment.

'I'll pray for Mathew,' he said. 'And I'll pray to get the telephone back so that Mr McCauley may be arrested before he burns the town down or tries to kill somebody else.'

Fr Devoy nodded.

'In the name of the Father,' he began, and heard Sweeny's voice join his, though quietly, unlike Sunday Mass. 'And of the Son, and of the Holy Spirit, Amen.'

He paused and tried to decide how to begin. He could launch into a rosary, but he thought that would be lazy, and unproductive. He asked the Lord for some help. It was the silent Lord, head bowed and bloody that he saw. Silence.

'Lord,' he began, and felt Sweeny looking at him, 'Grant us some silence in the midst of this storm. Allow us some peace in our hearts so that we may, with strength and humility, take your path through these troubled times.'

Troubled times. He must not slip into clichés.

'We do not know the hearts of other men, only their actions. It is for you therefore to judge, and for us only to beseech your guidance and your resolve and your courage. We pray for our brother Mathew, that his wounds are not serious and that he may, with your grace, make a full recovery. And we pray for our brother Hugo and our sister Helen, that their hands may be filled with your healing spirit and your love. We pray too for ourselves, that this humble priest and this, eh, policeman, Pat, Patrick, may be filled with your wisdom and courage and, eh, love, so that we may fulfil our responsibilities to this community. Amen.'

'Amen,' said Sweeny, with gravity.

'I think an Our Father, Pat, and maybe a couple of Hail Marys.'

'Right you are.'

Fr Devoy began the prayers, speaking softly, joined in murmur by the policeman, and he held in his mind the image of the crowning with thorns, and felt, with a great sense of relief, the lifting of his anxiety and the loosening of the knot in his chest and the lessening of his fear.

'. . . pray for us sinners, now and at the hour of our death. Amen.'

He blessed himself, and opened his eyes, and saw Sweeny staring at the table top, as if he too, had been granted his petition and felt now a calm inside, with which he might better deal with these troubled times. Troubled times. Fr Devoy considered the paucity of his devotional language. He should read more widely. Speak more directly to God. Perhaps then God would speak more directly to him.

At that moment Helen came into the room, clutching an empty candlestick, and with a strange, distracted look on her face. With a sudden rush that he could almost hear, Fr Devoy's fear returned.

'Is everything all right?' he said, in a hoarse whisper.

'Yes.'

Her eyes did not look at him. She was like a shocked person, one who had just walked from a car crash.

'Is he conscious?' Sweeny asked her.

'I don't know.'

'Did he say anything?'

'Yes.'

Sweeny immediately walked past her to the surgery, and Fr Devoy felt a deep unease, left alone with her. He could not say why. Her expression frightened him. In his chest he felt the familiar tangle return, the tightness that clutched at his breathing, that spun his head slightly.

'Are you all right?' he asked, and he was not sure to whom the question was addressed, coming as it did unbidden from his lips. There was a noise that startled him. It was his chair, scraping along the stone floor as he stood up.

'Yes.'

'Can I get you anything?'

'No, thank you.'

She was like a sleep walker, a ghost. Her eyes were fixed, staring into space. Her skin was pale and her hands seemed to twitch.

Fr Devoy felt an urge to flee her presence, afraid that she would turn on him in some way, in anger or entreaty. He was not prepared for either. He could tell her nothing of dead horses. He should sit with her, comfort her, talk gently with her about the inconstancy of human nature and the rewards of forgiveness. But her face was hard. She would not hear him. It was as Hugo had said. She was private with her grief. He should leave her to it.

'I'll go and see Mathew, I think,' he said, moving past her, feeling the tension that surrounded her small frame like the shimmering that surrounds the flames of candles. 'They may need me there.'

She made no response, and he moved with relief into the small corridor that led to the surgery, and only when he clutched the door handle and was about to go in did he pause, and wonder, and look back. The door to the kitchen had swung closed and he could not see her. As a boy he had had a dog, a mongrel called Kite, who had disappeared. He tried to remember what he had felt.

It was not the same. He turned and went through the door.

Dr Brooks stood by the sink, washing his hands in the flickering light, and glanced up at Fr Devoy and nodded.

Garda Sweeny stood by the low bed rubbing his chin, looking down at Mathew.

'How is he?' Fr Devoy asked.

'He's asleep. He's had a fright, and seven stitches, but he's fine. I doubt there's any fracture.'

'Can't you tell?'

'Not without an X-ray, not really.'

'You should have let me stay doctor,' said Sweeny, moving away from the bed. 'You really should.'

'I doubt he'd have talked if you'd been here, Pat. You know the way he is.'

'Indeed I do. Never heard an intelligent word out of his mouth. If it wasn't that it was yourself and Fr Devoy told me so I wouldn't believe he was capable of it.'

Dr Brooks nodded. Fr Devoy moved over to the bed and looked down at the sleeping face. Mathew's lips moved slightly, and his breathing rasped a little in his throat. But he was pale and still and dead looking, his gaunt features exaggerated in the candlelight, his matted black hair thrown across his forehead like seaweed on a beach, his thin arms and bony hands resting above the blankets, limp and cold.

'What did he say?' Sweeny asked.

Dr Brooks sighed, scratched his eyebrow and plunged his hands deep into his pockets.

'He confirmed that it was Brian McCauley who lit the fire at the cinema, with the help of Brennan and Higgins, and that it was McCauley who attacked him tonight.'

He looked at Fr Devoy.

'Apparently your conversation was overheard, John.'

'My God.'

He thought of the kitchen where he and Mathew had talked, of the garden outside, to which access could be easily gained. He pictured it. A shadow by the wall, crouching in the rain.

'And the boy?' asked Sweeny. 'What were they doing with the child?'

'A form of babysitting, apparently.'

As he listened to Hugo's account of Mathew's story, Fr Devoy kept his eyes on the sleeping figure, his body distinct and fragile beneath the blanket, like a vision of Christ laid out in the tomb. But Mathew was not like Christ. He breathed with an open mouth, spittle on his lips, and now and then his hands twitched.

Hugo's soft voice drifted through the room, and it seemed to Fr Devoy that he left something out, protecting Mathew by translation. It was a short tale. Sweeny took some notes, and made noises, satisfied and dissatisfied.

'I'll have to talk to him myself,' he said, when Hugo was finished. 'I'll leave it till tomorrow. I suppose you'll keep him here, doctor?'

'Yes, of course.'

'Right.'

There was a silence, and Fr Devoy watched the barely perceptible rise and fall of Mathew's chest. In the candlelight and the quiet he felt suddenly uncomfortable, as if he were watching the death of a man.

'Will he be all right?' he asked.

'He'll be fine,' said Hugo gently.

There was a still moment, and Fr Devoy made of it a kind of prayer, wordless, in the shadows of his mind where he could sense it and direct it upwards, but could not control it, or claim it for himself. His soul reached for God, and he felt it stretching. Then there was a kind of roar, and he did not know what it was until he heard the rain against the small windows and remembered the storm. It had returned to them while they talked, and he had not noticed it. It sounded now as strong as ever.

'Let's move to the kitchen,' said Hugo. 'We could all do with some tea I think.'

'There'll be no time for that, doctor,' said Sweeny. 'I've a man to arrest.'

Fr Devoy looked up at the policeman. His face wore a mask of determination that might have been issued with the uniform. A smile seemed to hover behind it.

Hugo sighed and motioned them into the kitchen. He blew out candles, leaving one night light on his desk, and the three men left the room like puppets, smaller than their shadows.

'The storm is worse,' said Dr Brooks, sitting at the table and reaching for his pipe. 'I don't see the point in going out in it. You should wait until the telephone is back, and organize someone to come in the car.'

'That could be hours, doctor.'

'Well, still. You can't go and arrest him by yourself. He might be dangerous.'

'I agree,' said Sweeny, and now he did smile. 'Which is why, if you don't mind gentlemen, I'll ask you both to come along.'

Fr Devoy and Dr Brooks looked at each other.

'Even with three of us,' said Fr Devoy carefully, 'if he becomes violent . . .'

'We'll call in for Dan Hartigan on the way.'

'I can't leave Mathew,' said Dr Brooks.

'Miss Helen is well able to look after him.'

'It's ridiculous,' said Fr Devoy. 'It's too dangerous. Why can't you leave it until tomorrow?'

'Because it's too dangerous to leave until tomorrow. I'd be falling down in my duties, Father, if I left it any longer at all. There's an arsonist and an attempted murderer loose in the night. I'm honour bound to bring him in.'

'You're being an awful pompous fool, Pat.'

'I resent that comment, doctor. I am simply doing my job.'

Dr Brooks slammed the table angrily.

'Oh for God's sake, Pat. Off you go then and do your job. It's not my job, nor John's, so we'll stay here, thank you very much.'

Sweeny looked at the doctor with astonishment, glanced at Fr Devoy, started to say something, stopped, swallowed, tugged at his jacket and walked brusquely towards the hall.

'Ah Pat, hold on,' said Dr Brooks apologetically. 'I'm sorry. Come here, Pat.'

But the policeman walked through to the hall without stopping. Fr Devoy looked at the doctor and made a face.

'Well, I can't help it,' said Hugo. 'The man's being a fool.'

'There's no need to tell him.'

The priest followed the policeman. He had stopped in the gloom by the front door. Lightning flashed and lit the high space briefly, and Fr Devoy was startled by a minor revelation, and by the strength of the darkness which followed.

Sweeney lifted the telephone receiver and put it down again. He circled the hall for a few moments and walked past Fr Devoy and back in to the kitchen.

'I may be a fool,' he said, going through the door, 'but I'm not such a fool that I'd go and arrest him by myself. The telephone is dead.'

Fr Devoy came after him. His thoughts were stirred. A new fear was risen. He was tempted, horribly tempted, to say nothing.

65

'We'll wait then,' said Dr Brooks, setting about lighting his pipe. 'Put the pot on the gas stove, will you, John?'

'Is Miss Helen in her room, doctor?' asked the priest.

'I assume so. Why?'

'Her coat is gone from the banisters.'

There was a long pause and the three men looked at each other silently. Then Dr Brooks stood and hurried out to the hall and called his daughter's name loudly.

'Helen! Helen? Are you up there?'

There was the sound then of the doctor running upstairs.

'Where'd she be gone at this hour?' Sweeny asked.

Fr Devoy stared at the policeman, and it was as if the question cleared his mind, and from the confusion and the vague terror that swirled through his thinking, formed the answer.

'McCauley's,' he breathed, and the sound of it chilled him.

Sweeny smiled incredulously, and was about to speak, but then Fr Devoy saw his mind begin to work, and his smile disappeared and his head dropped slightly and his mouth closed.

'Her bloody horses,' he said. 'She'll get herself killed.'

There was noise on the stairs and running in the hall and Dr Brooks came through the door, and it was plain to see that he had just gone through the same confused and terrible process, and had reached the same conclusion. He was pale, and he was frightened.

'She's gone. I have to . . .'

He did not finish. He turned and left the room again. Fr Devoy and Garda Sweeny followed him and watched as he hesitated in the centre of the hall and spun a little, confused, and ran then, past them, back through the kitchen and into the surgery. He emerged a moment later clutching his coat and hat.

'Sweeny, you come with me. John, you stay here and watch Mathew. He's asleep.'

'I'd rather go with you, Hugo,' said Fr Devoy, without really knowing his reasons. He was concerned about Helen, but he was nervous as well about staying in the house alone with Mathew.

Dr Brooks made no answer. He pulled on his coat.

'Bloody car. Why does no one have a car?'

'We could go up to the village and get some men and the car too,' said Sweeny.

'There's no time.'

'She might not . . .' Fr Devoy started, but Dr Brooks ignored him, and he fell silent. He pulled on his coat and watched Sweeny, guessing that the policeman wanted to get his cape but knew that such delay would not be tolerated. He looked around himself, as if expecting to find a spare coat close to hand.

Dr Brooks opened the front door and the three men went out into the rain. It was not as hard as it had been. The doctor set off immediately towards the road, shouting as he went.

'Helen! Helen!'

'Will we call for Dan Hartigan?' asked Sweeny.

'There's no time,' said Dr Brooks, his voice cracking with fear, or perhaps with the exertion of shouting. He broke into a run down the driveway.

Fr Devoy felt the rain on his head and glanced at the huddled figure of Garda Sweeny who jogged along beside him. He wondered whether he should also call out. He was fearful of his voice against the storm, afraid of being swept up in the doctor's panic, terrified that what they all feared was true.

'Helen!' screamed the doctor, and had his daughter's name crushed by thunder. A lightning flash split the darkness like a tear in a black curtain, and revealed briefly the trees that edged the road, and the flooding that had begun by the verges, and the way that they had to go, away from the village, along the sodden lanes, towards the farmhouse where Brian McCauley lived alone. Fr Devoy half expected, in that sudden light, to see some trail, some clue that Helen had indeed set off for McCauley's, but there was nothing but the rain and the colourless trees, and the road, before the curtain closed once more, and there was darkness.

'I can't see a bloody thing,' said Sweeny.

'Helen!'

They made their way to McCauley's in a kind of blindness. Their only light was thrown at them from above and they cowered beneath it. They were led by the doctor's panic, at a pace that exhausted Fr Devoy and had Garda Sweeny panting. There was no space in the priest's mind for anything other than the task of staying on his feet and keeping up. Nothing was considered, no thought given to what they might do when they got there, no plan made, no words exchanged, no communication other than the fear that crackled between them like a lightning strike caught in the nightmare parts of their minds.

They passed the place where they had found Mathew. Garda Sweeny paused and looked for the iron bar but could not find it. Fr Devoy saw his umbrella but thought it would be ridiculous to pick it up. They raced on.

They took the turn to McCauley's and found themselves in mud, slipping and stumbling. Sweeny cursed as Dr Brooks splattered him, his shoes smacking the mire as if he was attempting, by sheer force, to find solid ground beneath. Fr Devoy went down on one knee and tried to think of Jesus. But the muddy hands that pushed him up distracted him. They were his own, and he could think only of the dirt, and the rain on his head, and the mess this would make of his clothes.

'Helen!' shouted Dr Brooks, but quieter now, allowing the thunder to drown him out.

In the distance, on the high ground of his poor land, McCauley's cluster of buildings stood out black and definite against the flash of the sky. There was a light in a window of the house. A dog was barking insanely.

They hurried on, Dr Brooks moving as if his imagination was already inside, and his body lagged behind. He seemed to moan, and Fr Devoy watched his unsteady feet propel him like a man running downhill instead of up, and saw his flailing arms, and the despair in the craning of his neck and the angle of his head.

'God. Helen,' he groaned. 'Helen.'

They reached the barn first, where the dog seemed to be. His barking was hoarse and terrorized, and Fr Devoy thought it a sign of something horrible having happened, before he realized that it was the storm, the thunder and lightning, which had him in this state.

They stumbled into a yard where the shapes of various pieces of dilapidated equipment made grotesque shadows in the light thrown from the window nearest the door. They stopped, and it seemed to Fr Devoy that Dr Brooks now considered, for the first time, that it might not be as they had feared. He turned and looked at the other two, and there was doubt in his eyes.

'We are here for Helen,' he said, looking at Sweeny.

'Nothing else. I want to find my daughter. If she is not here then we're leaving. There'll be no arrests, Pat.'

The policeman was silent for a moment.

'We'll see how things go,' he said.

Dr Brooks nodded and stepped up to the door and knocked. The noise of the storm drowned him out and he knocked again, louder. He waited, and knocked again, louder still.

'McCauley! McCauley! It's Hugo Brooks, McCauley! I'm looking for my daughter. Open up for God's sake.'

He hammered on the door now, while Sweeny pressed cupped hands up against the window and peered in.

'There's a fire lit, and candles. But no sign of anybody.'

'McCauley!'

Sweeny stepped away from the window and towards Dr Brooks.

'Try the door, doctor.'

Dr Brooks looked at him, hesitated for a moment, and pushed down the handle. The door opened, and Fr Devoy felt a chill deep in his stomach spread up through his body as if he had stepped into water. Dr Brooks barely paused before moving over the threshold, followed closely by Garda Sweeny. Fr Devoy was more hesitant. He looked around the yard, back towards the barn where the dog continued to tear through the noise of the storm, at the hill down to the road, lit now by a double flash that made him wince. He turned and ducked his head instinctively and followed the others into the house.

Sweeny emerged from the small kitchen where the fire was lit, with two candles, handing one to Fr Devoy. Dr Brooks meanwhile stood in the small hall, peering about him quietly.

'Hello?' called Garda Sweeny. 'Is anybody here?'

He moved forward, holding out the candle in front of him. There was a door on his left which he pushed open gently. He stepped into the room and Fr Devoy, standing behind Dr Brooks caught a glimpse of a cluttered store room of some kind, with sacks on the floor and crowded shelves around the walls. Sweeny re-emerged and called out again, 'Hello? Is there anyone here?'

He moved ahead to the next door, on the right. He opened it and went through, followed by Dr Brooks. There was a moment of silence, and then a gasp, and Fr Devoy heard a gurgle in the throat of Garda Sweeny and a curse. He tried to look over Dr Brooks' shoulder, but could see nothing.

'Dear God,' said the doctor, his voice ragged.

Fr Devoy put his hand on his friend's arm and moved him gently. In the dim light, bolstered slightly now by his candle, he saw a tidy sitting room with a threadbare carpet. Above a fireplace there was a photograph of a woman. In one corner there was a valve radio. On a small table there was a bottle of whiskey and a glass. Fr Devoy thought at first that the whiskey was spilled, that the figure of Brian McCauley that sat in the chair, head thrown back, some kind of scarf around his neck, had fallen asleep, and spilled his whiskey all down his front and onto the chair and the table top. He glanced at the doctor and saw that this was not the case. He looked again, lifting his candle higher and catching for the first time the smell. It was not a scarf around McCauley's neck. It was a gap in his skin, a black space where flesh should have been, a gaping wound, a severance. He was covered in blood. His chest and stomach and legs were all drenched. The blood covered his arms and dripped from his dead hands into small puddles on the floor. It lay in pools on the table top and was spattered on the carpet beyond. Following the path of it with his eyes, Fr Devoy looked at the floor at his feet, and behind him, and at the skirting and up on the wall, and along the wall in an arc, a dripping arc like the splash of water on a dry roadside.

He gagged, and clutched his mouth. His candle fell, and there was a small hiss and the flame died. Sweeny shook and stepped back, past them, out to the hall. In the darkness Fr Devoy could just make out the shape of Hugo Brooks, his large shadow still and unmoving in the centre of the room. The thunder seemed to hush a little, as if the storm was shocked. Only the dog, frenzied, mad, continued as he had before.

'There are footsteps in the blood,' said Dr Brooks quietly, in his damaged voice. He turned then, and brushed past Fr Devoy, and stood in the light of Sweeny's shaking candle. His face was white, and his eyes streamed. His shoulders clenched and his throat contracted and he let out of him a roar so filled with pain that Fr Devoy stepped back and slipped on the slick floor and put a hand out to the wall to steady himself. His hand slipped on blood.

'Helen,' screamed the doctor. 'Helen. Helen. Helen.'

He dived into a deep blue pool where yellow birds swooped and cut the water and perched then on the branches of leafy trees and sang to him. The water covered him and he could not tell whether it clung to him like clothes as he moved or whether the water he was touching was different every second to the water he had touched the second before. Then he thought of water, and wondered what the parts of water were. They were not just drops, or else the rain would be like the sea and the sea would be like a bag of ballbearings. He could not understand what water was and he thought of himself and wondered what the parts of himself were and could not understand that either. He thought of the birds again. Yellow birds like pale flames.

A noise woke him and his head hurt.

For a long time he didn't know where he was. He thought at first that he was inside a black bag that had a tiny hole in it over his left ear where he could glimpse the sunlight. But when he stretched out his hand there was nothing there so he wasn't inside a bag. Then his hand touched a wall and he thought he was inside a tunnel that led to the place where you go when you've been murdered, but on the other side of him there was no wall so he wasn't inside a tunnel. He thought then that he was in heaven and he was disappointed. He turned to look at the place where he thought he'd seen sunlight and found himself looking instead at a volcano on an island about eighty-seven thousand miles away on another planet. So he thought then that he was in a spaceship. But he stared at the volcano and thought that from a distance it looked like a little silver cup candle on a blue saucer. And then he thought that that was probably what it was. He saw the glass cabinet then at the foot of his bed, and the black cape that was stuck to his skin underneath his blanket and he began to remember that he'd been murdered by Mr McCauley and now he was dead in Dr Brooks's house.

He sat up. Mathew.

'Mathew,' he said, quietly, and heard his voice in the thin air of the surgery, and guessed that he had been woken by somebody coming in and going out again, either Helen or Hugo, to get something, or to check on him. But they'd been noisy. Clattering. Battering. Boom boom.

'Boom,' he said, and there was thunder.

Mathew laughed.

'Boom,' he said again, and there was more thunder. He laughed again.

'Boom boom boom,' he said, making gravelly noises in the back of his throat.

The thunder caught up with him and raced him for a minute and then clattered on ahead like something collapsing in the sky, crack and clatter and batter and boom.

He giggled.

'Oh mercy mercy me. Oh mercy mercy me.'

His head hurt but it was not so bad as it had been and he pushed back the blanket and the cape and swung his legs, gently now, out over the edge of the bed and put his feet on the cold floor and sat there talking with the thunder and laughing, thinking that maybe he was not very badly injured at all, only knocked out and bloodied like old Mrs Murtagh's dog that was called Peg and who had stayed out by the main road after Mrs Murtagh had died and threw itself at every car that was the same colour as the car that had carried Mrs Murtagh away. Black it was. A coffin car, the name of which escaped Mathew. Peg. That was the dog. An old Labrador bitch with bad hind legs and bad eyes and a great good bark on her that'd wake the dead who go to ground in a hearse. Hearse. What had happened to Peg? He didn't know. Her bad hind legs meant her leaping wasn't forceful, only sad and sorry and hard to watch. She had been knocked out and bloodied and he had carried her to O'Connor's the vet's. He couldn't remember now what had happened after that. She had probably been destroyed.

'Destroyed,' he said, and the thunder said it back to him.

He put his hand to his head and felt a plaster or something close to where the pain was. He pressed on it to find out where the edges were, but it hurt too much.

He was very thirsty and a little cold. He didn't want to walk through Dr Brooks's house without a shirt on him. He thought for a moment and picked up the policeman's cape.

74

It was wet and black and smelled a little of old clothes and tea. He put it down again. He picked up a blanket and wrapped it around himself and bunched it up on his shoulders and hooded it over his head and looked at himself in the mirror. He looked like the Virgin Mary. A bit.

In the corridor to the kitchen he was in darkness and the storm was louder. He could hear the rain hitting the windows in the waiting room. He tried the door but it was locked. He left the door of the surgery open so that he would be able to see where he was going. On the tall table by the flowerpot where the big green plant with the small pink flowers sat, there was a tall candlestick with a stubby red candle in it. He touched his finger to the wax at the top and felt it warm and soft.

He listened at the kitchen door for a moment and could hear nothing, only the rumble of the thunder and the wind. He opened the door gently and stuck his head inside. There was no one there. On the table there were two candles, and another on the sideboard near the sink. They were stick candles and one was standing on a saucer and Mathew tut-tutted and stepped into the room and closed the door behind him. He went to the sink and turned on the tap and cupped his hands and drank cold water from them and sighed with pleasure as the water filled his dry mouth and flowed down his throat into his stomach and then up some back way to his sore head, soothing it. He cupped his hands again and held cold water to his eyes.

He stepped from the kitchen into the hall and there were more candles there, but no sign of anybody.

'Dr Brooks!' he called. 'Miss Helen?'

There was no answer and he went back to the kitchen and sat down.

They had all gone off somewhere. They had all rushed

off, making noises and leaving the candles burning in the kitchen where they might start a fire.

He stood up.

McCauley. Mr McCauley was trying to murder him again, leaving him in a house full of candles. He scampered through to the surgery and blew out the candles there and ran back to the kitchen and blew out all the candles there and ran out of the hall and blew out all the candles there and ran out the front door and slammed it after him and ran down the driveway.

He ran fast but he didn't run that fast because he had to look around him to make sure that there was no one running after him, or waiting up ahead of him by the side of the road like Mr McCauley had done before. The rain was hard and his head hurt as he jogged, bouncing up and down, and there was lightning and thunder that confused him.

He turned right, towards the town, away from Mr McCauley's, and left the road near the Protestant church and cut across the GAA grounds and into the small wood by Scanlon's farm and he waited there for a while to see if he was followed. He was not. He could see candles lit in the windows of Scanlon's house, and thought he saw the children, their shadows looking out at the storm. Past the wood he skirted the edge of the road to Sally Gap and saw a car go by, but not one he knew. He doubled back then towards Dr Brooks's, but over the fields this time, coming in towards Hartigan's farm from the direction of the small lake. He saw her then.

She was sitting in the middle of Mr Hartigan's field, the one that had the old trough in it, where sometimes she had set jumps for her horses. She had set big jumps here where her father couldn't see her. Not like the little jumps they had set in their own field, just the height of a barrel on its side,

76

but big jumps, a whole barrel high, and three in a row sometimes. And Mathew had seen her here take the saddle from Gepetto and the helmet from her own head, and ride bareback like an Indian. She had done it then with Mountain Star as well, but Poppy hadn't liked it and Mathew had watched her fall off three times before giving up.

Now she sat by a red-and-white painted barrel that lay in the wet grass beside the poles and planks. Her head was uncovered and bowed, her legs pulled up in front of her, her arms resting on them, her hands clasped together. Mathew stood and looked at her, and he frowned and wondered. She was getting wet. She would catch a cold and become ill. Her father would be worried. But he wondered where her father was, and why the house was empty, and he knew that this was a special place for her, like the small lake was for him, and that it was good that she was here instead of other places.

He would give her the blanket.

He walked across the field slowly, in front of her where she would see him clearly. It was dark though. She might not recognize him.

'Ahem,' he said, bringing his hand to his mouth to be polite, and drowning out the sound of it. He coughed properly and Helen looked up.

'It's Mathew Doyle, Miss Helen. Hello. Sorry to bother you. You'll have a blanket.'

She said nothing, only looked at him. He went up to her and slipped the blanket from his shoulders and draped it around hers and sat down beside her. She was sitting on a plank. It was hard, but he supposed that she sat on it thinking that it would somehow be dryer than the ground. It was not. Though it was not muddy like the ground.

'I think it's not as bad now.'

77

'What is, Mathew?'

'The storm, Miss. I think it's setting off somewhere else.'

'Yes.'

He looked at the side of her head and he saw her hair matted and specked with something dark.

'There's blood in your hair, Miss.'

'I know. It's on my hands too, and all over my clothes. All over my clothes and underneath them on my skin. It's disgusting.'

Mathew thought her voice was different, as if she had been shouting or crying.

'Is it mine, Miss?'

'What?'

'The blood. Is it out of my head?'

'No.'

'It isn't yours, is it?'

'No,' she said and then looked up at him. 'Why are you not at home? At my home I mean? How's your head?'

'My head is fine.'

'Where's my father?'

'I don't know, Miss. I woke up and there was no one around and I was scared.'

She sighed and wiped her hands on the grass. The thunder was further away and the lightning lit nothing.

'He's probably out looking for me. He'll go to McCauley's probably. I miss my horses.'

She sobbed and Mathew lifted his hand to touch her but he didn't know where to touch her and he hesitated and she sniffed and rubbed a sleeve across her mouth and nose and looked up and Mathew dropped his hand.

'I used to come here with them. There were three of them. It's like a family, like three people, three children, all burned up in a fire and dead.'

'All dead,' said Mathew sadly.

'McCauley is dead.'

'Who?'

'McCauley. Mr McCauley.'

'Dead?'

'Yes. I was going to kill him but he'd killed himself.'

Mathew clicked his mouth and stared at the hair that hung down from over her brow, blocking out her eyes from his view.

'Oh mercy.'

In the dark Mathew put his hands together and in his mind he prayed a prayer that came to him like a daydream. He saw Mr McCauley with the iron bar, swinging at him and shouting. Then he saw him outside the cinema striking his match and calling out his wife's name. Dead now. Bloody.

'His blood,' he said, his voice thin as the rain.

'He was sitting in it. He had a picture of her on the mantelpiece. She was very pretty. There was a candle by her face but I knocked it over. I heard him.'

'You heard him die, Miss?'

'I heard him.'

'Setting off somewhere else.'

'He screamed. Roared. I thought he'd seen me coming, or heard me, and was roaring at me. I think he was still alive when I went into the room. There was a noise from him. He had no shoes on and there was a dog barking in the barn.'

Mathew scratched his head.

'Dogs bark for their masters and howl at storms. Who's to know?'

'He had cut his own throat,' she said softly, like it was special. Then she rasped out, 'Disgusting!' to show that she didn't think it was special.

Mathew pictured Mr McCauley's throat, stretched with shouting, and frowned.

'I stamped up that hill,' said Helen, rasping still, 'like a madwoman and I went into his house with my hands gripped around that iron bar that he used on you and I was going to beat the life out of him. I was going to kill him.'

Mathew opened his mouth and the rain fell into it.

'For me?'

She looked up at him and seemed puzzled.

'No. For my horses. I wanted to kill him for my horses.'

He nodded and she looked away again.

'I would have killed him,' she said. 'But the wanker had already done it. Poured blood over everything like a blessing, and made himself something that he wasn't.'

Mathew looked at the ground between his legs and thought for a moment and wondered what to say.

'It was his wife, Miss. He missed her. He wanted to go to her.'

'I know.'

'He loved her you see and she's dead so he can't be with her so he probably thought that if he was dead as well then they'd be in the same place.'

'I know.'

She was quiet and the rain hit off her shoes and trickled away to the ground.

'Why did he kill my horses?'

'I don't know, Miss. I don't know why he did that. I don't understand that at all. Maybe he'd just gone mad.'

Miss Helen looked upwards at the sky. The rain was light now, all the thunder far away and almost quiet.

They sat for a while without saying anything, just looking around them. The rain made no sound but for a light pitter patter against the barrel. The grass crackled softly with water, and the hedge behind them dripped. Mathew saw a star, but it was gone again. Then he saw another, before the clouds closed on it, and then a patch of clear black sky appeared in the distance and moved towards them, hazing over sometimes, shuffling its stars for others, growing a little bigger, blurred at the edges. The rain stopped.

'Where are my horses, Mathew?'

'Burned in the fire, Miss.'

'I know. But where are they now?'

Mathew was confused for a moment, thinking maybe that they'd been buried, but thinking then that if they were burned in a fire they'd be ashes now and ashes aren't buried, they blow away into the air.

'They're in the air,' he said. 'Up in the sky.'

'That's what I think too. They gallop there, and there's no end to the fields where they gallop. When you saw them did they look happy?'

Mathew didn't know what she was talking about. Then he remembered dying earlier in the evening and the sight of Miss Helen's horses whinnying and nodding their heads.

'I don't know how you tell if a horse is happy, Miss. But I think probably they were. They were happy, yes.'

Mathew's teeth rattled and he began to shiver. Miss Helen lifted the blanket and draped it over both of them and put her arm around his shoulders and they sat together, touching.

'Where did you come from, Mathew?'

'Helen, Miss Heaven. I mean, heaven, Miss Helen.'

'Yes, but were you born here? Have you always lived here?'

'I can't say, Miss. I remember the Garda before Garda Cullen, and Garda Cullen was here a hundred years, and I remember the priest before the priest before Fr Devoy. So I must have been here for a long time, and I can't remember being anywhere else and nobody knows the secret of me so I suppose I'm here longer than anyone and that makes me from here. I am.'

A light came on in Hartigan's farmhouse across the fields. Not candlelight but an electric light. Then another. Then from where they sat they could see the countryside around them become flecked with lights and the rectangles of windows and the shapes of dim houses and the glow of the town in the distance with its street lights and its hum, out from hiding with the storm gone.

'That's pretty,' said Mathew.

It was possible now to pick out Dr Brooks's house, and the road it was on. There was a car there, and then another that drove towards it from the town at a high speed and another that followed it and they went past it out towards McCauley's. In the far off could be heard the toy sound of a siren.

'Everything's back,' said Miss Helen.

They huddled close together and watched the lights of the world that had come on and that rushed to and fro and wailed and shouted. They heard Helen's name called and Mathew looked at her, but she made no sign that she had heard or that it mattered.

'What is the secret of you, Mathew?'

'I'm not sure. I can't remember.'

'What has it to do with?'

'Pardon?'

'What kind of secret is it?'

'To do with confusion.'

'What do you mean?'

'I did not know my mother.'

'That's your secret?'

'That is the only secret I know, Miss Helen.'

'I don't see how that's a secret.'

'It is.'

'Is it?'

'It's a secret who she is.'

'Oh.'

'That is the secret of me.'

There were men on the fields between Dr Brooks's and Mr McCauley's. They made their way slowly, swinging the bright beams of torches and shouting, calling the name of Miss Helen. Dr Brooks's own voice was loud amongst them.

'What is the secret of you, Miss Helen?'

She looked at him and he saw a stain of mud or blood on her forehead where he had not seen it before. Her hair was matted and her face pale and her lips were thin and bitten. She smiled at him and shook her head.

'Dying, I think.'

Mathew nodded.

'That is the secret of most people,' he said. 'Dying and not dying.'

The searchers came closer, past the Hartigan's farmhouse, wheeling across the fields with their long light, picking out hedges and walls and gates and hay bales. Dr Brooks's voice called his daughter's name, and Garda Sweeny called out, 'Hello, hello' and Fr Devoy was silent, but his big bald head could be seen reflecting light like the moon.

There were other men too, and they formed a line and walked slowly over the field where Mathew and Miss Helen sat huddled on a plank by the leftovers of the horses who were dead and in the sky.

The men walked on, missing them.